THE SONG OF KAHUNSHA

Also by Anosh Irani

Fiction

The Cripple and His Talismans

ANOSH IRANI

THE SONG OF KAHUNSHA

MILKWEED
EDITIONS

© 2007, Text by Anosh Irani

Published 2007 by Milkweed Editions
Printed in Canada
Jacket design by CS Richardson.
Interior design by CS Richardson. Typeset in Mrs. Eaves.
Author photo by Tushna Shroff
07 08 09 10 11   5 4 3 2 1
First Hardcover Edition

ISBN-13: 978-1-57131-062-0
ISBN-10: 1-57131-062-2

Milkweed Editions, a nonprofit publisher, gratefully acknowledges sustaining support from Emilie and Henry Buchwald; the Bush Foundation; the Patrick and Aimee Butler Family Foundation; CarVal Investors; the Timothy and Tara Clark Family Charitable Fund; the Dougherty Family Foundation; the Ecolab Foundation; the General Mills Foundation; the Claire Giannini Fund; John and Joanne Gordon; William and Jeanne Grandy; the Jerome Foundation; Dorothy Kaplan Light and Ernest Light; Constance B. Kunin; Marshall BankFirst Corp.; Sanders and Tasha Marvin; the May Department Stores Company Foundation; the McKnight Foundation; a grant from the Minnesota State Arts Board, through an appropriation by the Minnesota State Legislature, a grant from the National Endowment for the Arts, and private funders; an award from the National Endowment for the Arts, which believes that a great nation deserves great art; the Navarre Corporation; Debbie Reynolds; the St. Paul Travelers Foundation; Ellen and Sheldon Sturgis; the Target Foundation; the Gertrude Sexton Thompson Charitable Trust (George R. A. Johnson, Trustee); the James R. Thorpe Foundation; the Toro Foundation; Moira and John Turner; United Parcel Service; Joanne and Phil Von Blon; Kathleen and Bill Wanner; Serene and Christopher Warren; the W. M. Foundation; and the Xcel Energy Foundation.

Library of Congress Cataloging-in-Publication Data
Irani, Anosh, 1974-
 The song of Kahunsha / Anosh Irani. -- 1st ed.
  p. cm.
 ISBN-13: 978-1-57131-062-0 (acid-free paper)
 ISBN-10: 1-57131-062-2 (acid-free paper)
1. Boys—Fiction. 2. Orphans—Fiction. 3. East Indians—
Fiction. 4. Bombay (India)—Fiction. I. Title.
PR9199.4.I73S66 2007
813'.6--DC22
2006034773

FOR MY PARENTS

ADI AND MAHRUKH IRANI

Without warning, the man rams the iron rod into the face that peers through the window. There is a sickening crunch and the face disappears. That must be Hanif the taxiwala, thinks Chamdi. The man stands guard outside the window, the iron rod by his side. He looks ready to repeat his actions should the need arise.

In the darkness of the lane, Chamdi can hear a woman scream from inside the blue shack. He imagines Hanif lying on the ground, his teeth smashed with an iron rod, blood streaming from his nose and mouth, while his wife bangs on the bolted door with her fists.

Chamdi is unable to move. None of the neighbours come to the family's rescue. Most of the men and women return to their shacks, and the few that remain outside look just as terrified as Chamdi.

Chamdi stares at Anand Bhai, who stands rooted to the ground. Dressed in black, Anand Bhai looks like he is part of the night itself. Chamdi cannot understand how Anand Bhai can smile at a time like this.

ONE

Chamdi runs his hands across his ribs.

He tries to push his ribs in, but it is of no use. They continue to stick out of his white vest. Perhaps it is because he is only ten years old. When he grows older, he will have more flesh on his body and his ribs will be less visible. With this thought, he walks down the steps of the orphanage.

He stands barefoot in the courtyard. He never wears slippers because he likes to feel hot earth against his feet. It is early January, and the rains are still far away. Even though a new year has begun, the earth looks old, the cracks in its skin deeper than ever. The sun hits Chamdi's black hair and forces him to squint.

He stretches his arms out and walks towards a wall, where his world ends and someone else's begins. As he nears the wall, he hears the city— faraway car horns, the hum of scooters and motorcycles. He knows Bombay is much louder than this, but the courtyard is not near the main road. Beyond the wall is a small marketplace where women sell fish and vegetables from cane baskets and men squat on their haunches and clean people's ears for a few rupees.

Pigeons sit in a row on the wall and chatter. Spikes of glass are placed along the edge of the wall to prevent people from entering the court- yard. Chamdi asks himself why anyone would bother sneaking into the courtyard. There is nothing to steal at the orphanage.

A loud cycle ring causes a few pigeons to flutter away, but they quickly regain their places on the wall. The shards of glass do not seem to bother the pigeons. They know where to place their feet.

Chamdi touches the wall and feels the black stone. He smiles when he thinks of the moss that will appear. Rain can make life out of walls. But it is still a few months before he can inhale deeply and take in his favourite scent. The smell of the first rains, that of a thankful earth satisfied by water, is what he dreams about all year long. If only the inside of the orphanage could smell like that, it would be the most loved orphanage in the entire city.

This tenth year has been hard for Chamdi. He is beginning to understand many things now. When he was a child, he had many questions, but now they might be answered, and he is afraid he will not like the answers at all.

He turns away from the wall and wanders towards a well made of grey cement.

As he stares at his reflection in the water, he wonders if he looks like his mother or like his father. He believes he has his mother's eyes, large and black. Was it his mother or father who dropped him off here? He wonders if they are alive.

He puts one foot on the parapet of the well.

Bougainvilleas surround him. They are his favourite flowers. So pink and red, full of love, he thinks. If these flowers were human they would be the most beautiful people on earth.

He puts his other foot on the parapet of the well and stands tall.

He looks through the open window of the orphanage. Most of the children are huddled together on one bed. He can hear them sing "Railgaadi." The girls make the *chook-chook* sound of a train, while the boys shout out the names of cities and towns at great speed—*Mandwa, Khandwa, Raipur, Jaipur, Talegaon, Malegaon, Vellur, Sholapur, Kolhapur.* There are so many places in India, Chamdi says to himself, and I have not visited a single one.

He likes how tall he feels with the added height of the parapet. Perhaps one day he will grow to this size. But it will still take years. And even if he does grow tall, so what? He will still have nowhere to go. There will come a day when he must leave the orphanage. But there will be no one to say goodbye to. No one will miss him if he goes.

He stares at the water in the well.

It is extremely still. He wonders if he should jump in. He will swallow as much water as his body will allow. If his parents ever come back for him, they will find him sleeping at the bottom of the well.

The moment he has this thought, he gets off the parapet.

He walks quickly towards the orphanage and climbs up the three steps that lead to the foyer, where the children's rubber slippers are placed in a neat row on the ground and a black umbrella hangs from a hook on a yellowed, patchy wall.

His small feet leave dirt marks on the stone floor. He enters the sleeping room and receives an angry look from Jyoti, who sits on her haunches and washes the floor. She always scolds him for not wearing slippers.

Twenty metal beds occupy this room. The beds are placed opposite each other, in rows of ten each. They have thin mattresses covered with white sheets but no pillows. Since Jyoti is mopping the floor, the children are on their beds. Most of them are still on a bed near the window and are playing a game of antakshari. They have stopped singing "Railgaadi" and are now at the point in the game where they need to sing a song that begins with the letter V.

Without taking her eyes off Chamdi, Jyoti dips a thick grey cloth into a bucket that contains a mixture of water and phenyl. She slaps the cloth onto the ground. Chamdi looks at her and smiles. She has worked at the orphanage for many years, along with her husband, Raman, and Chamdi knows she means no harm. He wishes Jyoti could stop and make tea for him, but she will do so for all the children only after she has finished washing the floor. She has put oil in her hair today, and the smell of oil and phenyl floats through the room.

Chamdi looks inside Jyoti's big green bucket, at the water dark with dirt, and he is reminded of the well. He looks away immediately, and heads for the prayer room. He assures himself that no one will know that he just thought of jumping into the well. No one except the man who stands in the prayer room like a beautiful giant.

Chamdi is unable to look at this man. Chamdi is ashamed of the thoughts he had, especially since this man has suffered more than anyone else Chamdi knows.

Jesus.

Even though Jesus' eyes must have seen so much cruelty when he was alive, they reveal none of it now. But what Chamdi likes best about Jesus is all that light around his head, as if Jesus invented electricity. When Chamdi burns because he sees another child who is happy, who has not just one parent but two whole parents, he thinks of how badly Jesus was treated. Jesus came to earth full of love, but he was sent back on a cross with blood and angry words.

It encourages Chamdi that Jesus was once a small boy too but then he went on to become a leader of men. Even though talking to Jesus does make him feel better, Chamdi is always uncomfortable when he asks for something. Each morning, all the children collect in this prayer room and, instead of praying, they close their eyes and make demands. Chamdi does not feel this is real prayer. To him, real prayer means sending a bright thought, like *Thank you* or *I love you*, to heaven. That is prayer. The moment you ask for something, the prayer room becomes a marketplace.

He looks around to see if anyone is watching him. He does not want anyone else to witness his prayer. Jesus has never answered him, but he understands that after the way Jesus was treated, he may not trust human beings at all. So he accepts Jesus' silence.

Chamdi tells Jesus that from now on, he will learn to carry sadness with him as if it is an extra toe. As he utters these words, he knows Jesus will be proud of him.

Chamdi feels tired and wants to rest, but at the same time he does not want Jesus to stop watching over him. So he lies down on the stone floor and sends his thoughts to Jesus: *I promise to try to be happy*.

Chamdi knows he is better off than blind people, or children with diseases, or even stray dogs with so many holes in their bodies.

He feels much better. Now he can close his eyes and do what he likes to do best, what he has been doing since the day he was born, or maybe since he was three years old. He will imagine the city of his birth, Bombay.

He has spent all his life inside the courtyard of the orphanage. He has not seen much of Bombay. And lately, what he has heard about Bombay has disturbed him. Mrs. Sadiq, who runs the orphanage, has not allowed any of the children to step outside the orphanage walls over the past three weeks.

The Hindus broke down the Babri Masjid, a mosque in Ayodhya, a faraway place, she said, and now Hindus and Muslims were hurting each other in Bombay because of that. The streets were not safe anymore, not even for children.

But Chamdi reminds himself that a new year has begun.

No more shops will be looted, no more taxis will be burned, no more people will be hurt. If these things truly happened, then Chamdi must rebuild Bombay on his own, brick by brick.

So he closes his eyes and sees a red rubber ball.

In Chamdi's Bombay, children play cricket in the street with a red rubber ball and even if the batsman hits the ball hard, sends it crashing into a windowpane and the glass breaks, no one gets angry. The glass mends itself in a few seconds, and the game resumes. The umpire is an old man who runs a cigarette shop. Even though he cannot pay attention because he has cigarettes, paan, and supari to sell, he is so gifted that he recreates the game, ball by ball, in his head. The spinner bowls in strange ways. He runs backwards and without even looking at the stumps, tosses the ball miles into the air, and the batsman, if he is experienced, waits patiently for the ball to land, which can take anywhere from one minute to seven minutes. When the ball does land, it spins so sharply that everyone feels giddy.

He sees people celebrating Holi. Everyone is out in the streets dancing to the beat of dhols, throwing coloured powder in the air, jumping into those colours and becoming them for a day or week. The people have finally understood the true nature of Holi—if their faces are dipped in green, then for the next few days Bombay is lush, and men, women, and children pass

through their troubles with ease. If their chests
are smeared in red, it means they will fall in love
and get married. Every colour known to man
comes to the people of Bombay as a friend, and
the people become them all.

But such a place must be known by another
name, he reasons. So he invents one, and says it out
loud: "*Kahunsha*." To him this means "the city of no
sadness." Someday all sadness will die, he believes,
and Bombay will be reborn as Kahunsha.

By the time he wakes up, he feels refreshed.

As he enters the sleeping room, he sees little
Pushpa, who sits on her bed with her head against
the wall. She breathes heavily because she has
asthma. Once, at night, she woke Chamdi up and
said she was dying. No one is going to die, Chamdi
replied, terrified because he could not do much.
So he patted Pushpa on her head and prayed to
Jesus, although he felt it was meaningless to pray
when she was not even allowed to breathe. After a
while he just sat there in the darkness and listened
to Pushpa gasping for air. Right now, Pushpa
twirls her hair and daydreams, and Chamdi is
pleased to see that she is not suffering.

The sleeping room is quite gloomy now, although a small amount of light spills in from the prayer room, which gets more sun. Chamdi looks at all the children who exist in this borrowed light. Our eyes show that we are orphans, he thinks. He tells himself that if he were to see any of these children years from now, as grownups, he would still be able to recognize them.

He turns his attention to Dhondu. Dhondu the ghost-boy who sleeps with one eye open. Even though Dhondu is the most well-built boy in the orphanage, he is terrified of ghosts. He believes that if he falls into a deep sleep, a ghost will enter his body, and he will be forced to spend the night outside his body like a scared spirit. At night, Dhondu speaks a strange language that he claims to have learned from the ghosts. He can hear them fight between themselves over who shall take his body first. On nights when there is not much to do, which is every other night, all the children watch in great delight as Dhondu is chased by ghosts.

Kaichi lies on the floor. Kaichi looks different from the rest of the children. He has green eyes and fair skin because he is from Nepal. Chamdi is thankful that Kaichi is asleep right now. Kaichi has earned the name because he always cuts into everyone else's conversations like a scissor. But right now, Kaichi is still as a stone. Chamdi steps over him.

The grandfather clock in the sleeping room strikes three, and it occurs to Chamdi that he missed lunch. It is not much of a lunch, a ball of rice and vegetables, but at least it fills his stomach. He wonders why no one came to the prayer room to wake him up, especially Mrs. Sadiq.

Besides Jesus, Mrs. Sadiq is perhaps the only person that Chamdi talks to openly. She has looked after Chamdi since he was an infant. But he does not trust her completely. He feels she is hiding something from him. All these years, she has fed him and bathed him, but there have been times when she has not been able to look him in the eye. He believes she knows something about his parents. One day he will find out.

Still, Chamdi is grateful for all that she has done for him. Mrs. Sadiq has taught all the children how to read and write. But she pays special attention to Chamdi. She once called him a "bright boy" in front of all the other children. It gave him a chance to explain that he was "bright" because he believed in the power of colours. *All of you should stand near the bougainvilleas each day*, he proudly announced. *Then you shall be bright like me*. But the children laughed as if Chamdi were mad. From that day, he decided to keep his secrets to himself.

He walks through the narrow corridor that leads to Mrs. Sadiq's office. A portrait of a Parsi lady hangs on the wall. For many years Chamdi thought this lady looked very stern. But one day Mrs. Sadiq told everyone who the Parsi lady was, and Chamdi changed his mind. The lady's name is H.P. Cama. When she was alive, the orphanage was her home. It was due to her kindness that the children have shelter today. Mrs. Sadiq taught all the children to thank "Lady Cama" each time they pass through the corridor. Chamdi does not thank her each and every time because sometimes he is in a hurry to get to the toilet, but he has told Jesus about Lady Cama: If you see her in heaven, please look after her.

Now Chamdi watches Mrs. Sadiq from the corridor.

She sits at a brown wooden desk and reads a letter through silver-framed glasses. Behind her, through the open window, Chamdi can see the bougainvilleas sway in the breeze. He likes the manner in which their red petals surround Mrs.

Sadiq's head, without her knowing, as though they are protecting her. She raises her head and looks at the clock on the wall, but she does not notice Chamdi. As she reads the letter again, the sun adds a tinge of light to her white hair.

Chamdi looks at her long, bony arms as they rest on the table and wonders how many children those hands cared for over the years. He knows that just as he longs to know his real mother and father, Mrs. Sadiq once longed for a child of her own. He overheard her talking to Jyoti one afternoon while the two of them sat on the orphanage steps and drank tea. It was one of the few occasions Chamdi had seen Mrs. Sadiq treat Jyoti as a friend instead of a servant.

Chamdi discovered that Mrs. Sadiq used to be married. Her husband disliked her working at the orphanage. He told her that if she could not have children of her own, there was no need to go look after someone else's. One day when she got home, he had packed her bags. He asked her to leave. So she picked up the little that she owned and took a taxi back to the orphanage. She never saw him after that day. Mrs. Sadiq thinks her husband could be dead by now because he was fifteen years older than her. That was all she said to Jyoti.

It surprised Chamdi that Mrs. Sadiq's life story could be told in only a few sentences. So he made up his mind to achieve something so wonderful that if he were to tell anyone his life story, it would take days to tell, even weeks, and the ending would be a happy one, unlike Mrs. Sadiq's. He wanted to tell Mrs. Sadiq about his plans, but she would have shouted at him for spying on her.

Mrs. Sadiq looks at the clock again. She runs her hands over her white hair, which is tied in a bun. She wears a blue sari and matching rubber chappals. Chamdi can always tell which room of the orphanage she is in from the *flip-flop* of her chappals. When she steps out of the orphanage, she wears leather sandals. The rubber chappals had made her slip in the rain once, and that is when she hurt her back. The bottle of Ayurvedic oil that she rubs on her back sits on the table next to a blue glass paperweight. Mrs. Sadiq holds the blue paperweight in her fist and then looks at the clock. Chamdi wonders if she thinks the clock and paperweight are connected.

She finally sees Chamdi standing in the corridor.

As she gets up from her wooden chair, the small green cushion that supports her lower back falls to the floor. She slowly bends to pick it up, but

Chamdi can tell from the strain on her face that her back hurts. So she lets the cushion remain on the floor. Chamdi enters the room, picks the cushion up, and places it against the back of Mrs. Sadiq's chair.

Mrs. Sadiq smiles at Chamdi, but he knows she is worried about something because a smile is not supposed to make a person look older. She walks to the window and rests her elbows on the sill. Chamdi looks out the window too, sees the well, and warns himself never to go near it again.

Chamdi and Mrs. Sadiq stand in silence and listen to the occasional car horn. He wonders what would happen if the orphanage were in the heart of Bombay. He would have to hear buses rumble in a mighty manner all day long. Jyoti has told him that the buses of Bombay have no respect for human beings. His own eyes have marked how cruel buses are to humans—they prevent people from getting on, and the people who do get on are forced to hang from the buses in the most dangerous manner. Jyoti also told him that when she came to Bombay from her village, there was no seat for her inside the bus, so she sat on the roof along with five men and travelled that way for a whole day. At the time Chamdi thought that he would love to sit on the roof of a bus and see all the villages of India.

But right now he wants to know what troubles Mrs. Sadiq because she has not said a word to him. Chamdi has noticed that in the last three months Mrs. Sadiq has grown quieter and quieter, and he wonders if it is a sign that she is dying. He is afraid to ask her. But he must make her talk because the more she speaks, the longer she will live.

Before Chamdi can ask her anything, Mrs. Sadiq pats him on the head, walks back to her table, and reads the letter again. She picks up the black telephone receiver and puts it to her ear as if to check whether it is working. Then she puts the receiver back in its cradle, takes her silver glasses off, and rubs her eyes.

Maybe she did not sleep last night, thinks Chamdi. Her eyes are red. But they could also be red from crying. He finds it strange that although tears are colourless, they make the eyes turn red. He has often wondered about his own eyes. If he stares at the bougainvilleas for days and days at a time, will his eyes acquire their colour? Then he would be the only boy in Bombay, or even the world, to have pink or red pupils.

The ring of the telephone snaps him out of his thoughts. Mrs. Sadiq does not answer it immediately. She lets it ring, and Chamdi knows that she wants him to leave. If she were his mother, he would have clung on to her leg and refused to go.

Before Chamdi leaves the room, he glimpses the bougainvilleas through the window and is pleased that the breeze makes them dance. It is a sign that Mrs. Sadiq will be okay.

TWO

Mrs. Sadiq scratches her right eyebrow with her thumbnail. After a few seconds, she moves on to the left. This is a habit Chamdi has noticed over the years. Whenever she is worried, she does this.

But he has never seen her worry so much about a simple telephone call. He knows she is holding something from him, just as she holds something from him when she refuses to tell him about his mother and father. But no matter how many times she tells him she knows nothing about his parents, he is determined to find out the truth. After all, it was Mrs. Sadiq who named him Chamdi—"a boy of thick skin."

Today Chamdi does thank Lady Cama as he passes her in the corridor. Chamdi knows it is not possible, but he feels her ears have grown larger. It could be because her ears are constantly filled with so many thank-yous. If this is true, then God must have the largest ears in the world.

Sonal, the oldest girl in the orphanage, stands looking out the window in the sleeping room. She wears a faded green dress that came with a set of old clothes donated by a Christian family that was moving to Madras. The brown shorts and white vest that Chamdi wears came from the same family. Chamdi envies the Christian boy whose waistline is wider than his. It means the boy eats much more than a ball of rice and vegetables. Chamdi wants to become a man fast. He wants to be strong. He knows that Sonal wants to grow up quickly too. She is hurt by the way she looks right now. Chamdi heard Mrs. Sadiq telling Sonal that girls take time to show their beauty. So Sonal now believes that she will be a beauty when she grows up. She is not sure at what age she will become beautiful, but she is willing to wait patiently.

In a corner of the room, three boys stand in a group and play koyba, the game of three white stones. Even though they are not brothers, these boys resemble each other. They are stout of chest but their legs are thin. Chamdi believes they look similar because they are always together. They do not talk much with the other children. One of the boys lifts his right leg as he releases the small round stone from his hand. It hits the stone on the floor with precision.

Now Chamdi sees Jyoti walk out the main door. It is still too early for her to go home, so he assumes she must be off to the market to buy vegetables or cooking oil for Mrs. Sadiq. Chamdi wonders what Mrs. Sadiq would do without Jyoti because Mrs. Sadiq does not have the strength to squat on the ground and scrub floors, or cook food for twenty children. Even though Jyoti's work is shoddy, she has not left the orphanage to work in someone's private home for a larger sum. Perhaps this is because of her husband, Raman. Chamdi knows that no household would employ a drunkard. At least here Raman cleans the toilets and then he is out of everyone's way. On some days he passes out in the courtyard and all the children gather around him and wonder if he is dead.

Just as Chamdi is about to walk down the steps and into the courtyard, he feels someone tug his hand. It is Pushpa. She holds in her hand an old, tattered copy of *Chandamama*, a children's storybook that contains fabulous tales like "The Child Who Ate a Mountain" and "The Flying Rhinoceros with Morals." Pushpa wants to speak, but she waits till she has enough air. Chamdi knows what she wants anyway. He takes the book from Pushpa's hand and walks with her to a corner of the room near a large wooden cupboard that contains the children's clothes and toys. The cupboard has a long mirror on one door and a pink flower tree painted in the wood on the other. There is a bird in one of the tree's branches. Chamdi loves this painting because it looks as though the bird's mouth is open and it is sending out a song that travels miles and miles.

They sit on the floor as far away as possible from the Koyba Boys. One of the boys has just won three games in a row and he is walking around with his chest out. The other two are upset that they are not winning, so they rub all three white stones together and kiss them for luck.

Chamdi likes it when Pushpa wants him to read a story to her. He never starts reading at the beginning of the book because he believes that he needs to open the book to the story that is meant to be read. As he looks at Pushpa, he notices again that even though she is tiny, and the youngest child in the orphanage, her eyes are large and round, much like the koyba stones.

Chamdi closes his eyes and opens the book to "The Hunger Princess." He knows this story and is happy it has been chosen. "The Hunger Princess" is a love story about a beautiful princess in ancient India who was not allowed to marry the boy of her choice, a poor farmer's son. So she decided to starve herself to death. The king did not think his daughter would do such a thing, but she bravely refused to eat, and such was the effect of her devotion that crops stopped growing and the whole kingdom starved until the king finally agreed to give his daughter to the poor farmer's son.

It was Mrs. Sadiq who first read this story to all the children. As Chamdi thinks back, he understands why the story gave Mrs. Sadiq no joy when she told it. Perhaps it made her real- ize how differently her own story had turned out, and even though the tone of her voice was gentle, Chamdi could tell that Mrs. Sadiq did not believe a word of what she was reading. He is sure of that now. But he is pleased that Pushpa is ready to wholeheartedly believe whatever she is told. After he reads her the story, he might reveal to her the power of colours. But just as he is about to start reading, Mrs. Sadiq steps into the room.

"I want all of you to sit on the floor," she says. "I have something important to tell you."

Chamdi closes the storybook and tells Pushpa that as soon as Mrs. Sadiq makes her announcement, he will start the tale. Pushpa takes the copy of *Chandamama* from Chamdi's hand and admires the illustration of the Hunger Princess, whose long black hair covers her face as she weeps for the poor farmer's son. Dhondu the ghost-boy sits down next to the two of them.

It is hard for the Koyba Boys to stop their game because one boy has now won four games in a row. He tells the others that he wants to set a record of five. But at a look from Mrs. Sadiq, they pick up one stone each and sit down next to Sonal, who is already waiting, her hand on her chin.

Chamdi catches Mrs. Sadiq's reflection in the mirror on the wooden cupboard. Her body is frail and the veins on her forehead are visible. She looks even more tired now than she did a while ago in her office. This means the news cannot be good.

He recalls the last time she made an announcement. It was regarding the Babri Masjid. The
mosque had been destroyed on December sixth,
the same day as Pushpa's birthday. She told them
about it a couple of days later, when riots had broken out in Bombay.

Over the next few days, Chamdi overheard
Raman tell Jyoti that it was unsafe for Mrs. Sadiq
to go out of the orphanage as well because she
was Muslim. Muslim-owned shops were being
looted and set ablaze. Muslim men, women and
children were being harmed, and the police
offered no protection at all. It was Raman who
suggested that Mrs. Sadiq wear a sari instead
of the traditional salwar kameez. If she did
step out, she might be able to pretend that she
is Hindu. But Chamdi did not want to believe
any of this. After all, Raman drank so much. It
made him tell lies.

Mrs. Sadiq's words bring Chamdi back to the
present.

"I have watched some of you come here as
babies, and now you are so heavy that I cannot
even lift you," she begins.

Her mouth breaks into a faint smile. She looks at
Sonal, who plays with the frills of her green dress.

Sonal often wanders off into Dreamland. It irritates Chamdi that Sonal is not paying attention.

"Sonal, you came here when you were two years old," says Mrs. Sadiq. "How old are you now?"

Sonal hears her name and looks up at Mrs. Sadiq. She raises her hand to answer. Mrs. Sadiq has taught them that when they are in a group they must raise their hand if they wish to speak.

"How old are you?" repeats Mrs. Sadiq.

"I'm nine years old," replies Sonal.

"We have one boy who will soon be a man," says Mrs. Sadiq. "Can anyone tell me who that is?"

Pushpa points to Chamdi. Chamdi looks down because he does not like the attention. What is so great about being born before the others? He has done nothing to achieve it.

"As you all know, this orphanage used to be owned by a Parsi lady," says Mrs. Sadiq. "H.P. Cama died thirty years ago. It is said that she had no husband, no children. She decided that after she died her home would be a home for little children like you."

Why is she telling us what we already know? thinks Chamdi. He is now sure that the news is bad because Mrs. Sadiq is wasting time and she looks at her feet as she talks.

"But there is a problem now."

Mrs. Sadiq straightens her back and head when she says this, but Chamdi knows this will not change the nature of her words.

"Three months ago, I received a letter. It was from the trustees of this orphanage . . . the people who are in charge of this place. A man showed up and he was able to prove to the trustees that he is H.P. Cama's grandson."

Mrs. Sadiq stares at her feet again. Then she crosses her arms and scratches her elbows.

"So the trustees are being forced to hand over the place to him, and they hear that he is going to construct a building in place of this orphanage. I begged them to provide some sort of shelter, even a smaller shelter would do, anywhere . . . They gave me a final answer at three o'clock today."

Beside Chamdi, Pushpa opens *Chandamama* and flips through the pages. She stops at an illustration of a young boy who holds a mountain in his hand and is ready to eat it. Pushpa looks at Chamdi, points to the boy's gaping mouth, and giggles. But Chamdi is concentrating hard on Mrs. Sadiq's words.

"The thing is, the trustees have asked us to leave this orphanage. We have one month to leave.

This orphanage will be broken down and a tall building will come in its place."

Suddenly, Chamdi is filled with anger at Mrs. Sadiq. She knew about this three months ago. Why did she not tell him? All she did was grow quieter and quieter as if her silence would help them. And what kind of people are these trustees? How can they choose a building over children?

"Tell them we will not leave," says Chamdi.

"We have no choice, Chamdi."

"This is our home."

"But they own it. There's nothing we can do. There are times in your life when you cannot do anything. We are lucky that we were allowed to stay in this place for so many years. There are people who are worse off on the streets."

"But that's where you are sending us."

"I'm not sending you anywhere. It's not up to me. But I'm doing all I can to find another place for you all."

"Where?"

"Pune."

"Where is that?"

"Pune is three hours from here by train. I know a priest there. His name is Father Braganza. He runs an orphanage too. I have written to him."

"We are leaving Bombay?"

"I have tried to find a place in Bombay but there is nothing. And I feel that the farther away you are from this city, the safer it is. These are dangerous times. You know how bad the month of December was. Some people say the riots are not over, that more fighting and looting will take place."

Chamdi does not like it when Mrs. Sadiq says this. Just because her life took a wrong turn does not mean theirs will too. And he has not seen any riots. He has seen Bombay in his mind and it is wonderful.

"What if Father Braganza says no?" asks Chamdi.

"He won't," she says. "Look—there's no point in talking about this now. We will find another place. For now, all we can do is pray."

Mrs. Sadiq runs her hands over her white hair and leads all the children to the prayer room. Pushpa leaves the storybook on the floor. Pushpa and Chamdi are the last to enter the prayer room.

Chamdi can tell that Mrs. Sadiq is scared. She usually stands just below Jesus and talks to the children before the prayer, but today she kneels alongside them. With her head bent down, she softly says, "Tell Jesus everything."

Chamdi loses track of how long they stay silent, but by the end of the prayer it feels as if all the children have moved a little closer to each other.

Mrs. Sadiq is the first to stand up. All the children walk past her out of the prayer room. No one says a word. As Pushpa passes Mrs. Sadiq, she pulls on Mrs. Sadiq's hand, as though she does not want to go to the next room alone. But Mrs. Sadiq does not leave. Chamdi is last in line and he has been looking at her. Mrs. Sadiq tells Pushpa to carry on.

Chamdi is burning with anger because he has heard the truth. And he has decided that if Mrs. Sadiq can speak the truth with such ease today, she will tell him what she has been hiding from him for all these years.

"You have to tell me the truth," he says.

"I did tell you the truth," Mrs. Sadiq replies. "We have no home now."

"Not about the orphanage. I want the truth about me."

"Chamdi, I've told you many times. I know nothing."

"You're lying."

"I know nothing. I promise."

"Swear by Jesus," insists Chamdi.

"I have done that for you also. Many times." Mrs. Sadiq sighs.

"Put your hand on Jesus. Then say it."

Chamdi knows that in the past Mrs. Sadiq has lied to him. She has sworn by Jesus that she knows nothing about his mother or father, but she has never placed her hand on Jesus and lied. Mrs. Sadiq touches Jesus' feet.

"I know nothing about your mother and father," she says.

"You're still lying."

"What makes you think that?"

"You removed your hand from Jesus' feet while you were saying it."

"Chamdi . . . you must stop asking about your parents."

"Then I will ask you something else."

"That's better."

"Do you remember when you asked me if I kicked one of the Koyba Boys while he was sleeping?"

"I remember."

"What did I tell you?"

"You told me you did kick one of them."

"And you know why I told you? Because I'm a bad liar. Just like you. Tell me, please. Please, Mrs. Sadiq, I need to know about my parents."

"But what's the use now?"

"I will stop thinking about them. Some nights I wonder if they lost me by accident and are still searching for me."

"Chamdi, it's harmful to keep dreaming like this."

"Then tell me the truth."

There is a long silence. Chamdi expects that Mrs. Sadiq will break the silence by telling him for the hundredth time that she knows nothing about his mother and father.

"Mrs. Sadiq, you kept silent for three months about the letter, and you did not tell us we were going to lose our home, and now see the end result."

"Chamdi . . ."

"I know why you're sending us to Pune."

"What do you mean?"

"You don't want to look after us anymore."

Chamdi looks directly at Mrs. Sadiq when he says this. There is disbelief on her face. Chamdi has never spoken to her in this manner before.

"Chamdi . . . there's nothing I can do. It's not up to me. The trustees are in charge. I've told you the truth. I promise."

"Then tell me the truth about my parents also."

"You might not like what you hear."

"Tell me."

"Think hard about what you ask."

Chamdi wants to tell Mrs. Sadiq that he has spent his whole life thinking about this. On some nights he stands by the open window of the orphanage and begs his parents to come back for him, but he does it only on nights when there is a strong wind so that the wind can carry his words to them. Sometimes he stares at himself in the mirror and wonders what part of his face his parents did not like. He wants to tell Mrs. Sadiq why he stands in the courtyard all day. It is because he had a dream once that he was standing in the courtyard and a man and woman walked towards him, and he suddenly started running to them because his heart recognized who they were, and he was in their arms within seconds, and the whole courtyard was happy for him, especially the bougainvilleas . . .

"Your father left you here, Chamdi," Mrs. Sadiq says sharply. "He's never coming back. I thought it was better for you not to know."

Chamdi is shocked at the manner in which Mrs. Sadiq's words jump out. She takes a few steps to the window and looks out into the courtyard.

She takes her glasses off and clasps her hands behind her back. She continues slowly.

"I saw your father," she says. "I saw your father the day he left you. It was in the afternoon and I had just finished eating. We had a dog called Rani, who is gone now. Rani was a very gentle dog. But Rani started barking, and she would bark only if someone was running. For some reason Rani never liked people running. She never ran herself. Even though dogs love to run and chase things, my Rani never ran. She was like a queen, always walking."

"What did you see?" asks Chamdi.

"I walked to the window and saw a man running. He was running away from the orphanage."

"What did he look like?"

"He was running away from the orphanage and I had a sick feeling in my heart. The same sick feeling I get every time someone leaves a child here. It's a feeling that never goes away."

"What did the man look like, Mrs. Sadiq?"

"I looked at the man and then back at Rani, who was barking loudly. She was near the well and next to her was a white bundle. That white bundle was you."

"What did the man look like?" This is what I

want to know, thinks Chamdi. Tell me what he looks like.

"He looked scared. I never saw his face. I could only see his back, but even from his back I could tell that he was scared."

"Was that my father?"

"Yes."

"But how do you know?"

"I could tell by the way he ran."

"What do you mean, Mrs. Sadiq?"

Mrs. Sadiq sighs. "The way he ran, Chamdi. It could mean anything. It could mean that he loved you very much but was forced to leave you alone and was running from you because it would be impossible for him to simply walk. Or it could mean that he ran because he was afraid of being caught. You must decide what it means."

"Did you see his face?"

"No."

"Are you sure?"

"No."

"You mean you *saw* his face?"

"The thing is, Chamdi . . . I saw his back so clearly that over the years his face slowly started forming, and in my mind he had the same face that every man in this world has. His face was the same face as that of my husband, it was the same face as that of the man who sells vegetables around the corner, it was the same face . . . and the face does not matter at all."

"Mrs. Sadiq, I don't understand what you are saying."

"I'm saying that I did not see his face. I'm sorry."

Why did she not see his face? Chamdi asks himself. That was the most important part.

"But there's something else," Mrs. Sadiq says. "I still have the white cloth that you came in. Do you want it?"

"The white cloth?"

"You should have it. See it once and for all. I'll be right back."

As Chamdi waits, he caresses the nails in Jesus' feet. He looks at Jesus' face for a sign of life, but there is nothing.

Mrs. Sadiq stands in front of Chamdi again. She holds in her hand a white cloth. There is nothing special about it at all, thinks Chamdi. It is just a white cloth crumpled in an old woman's hand.

"This is what you came in," she says.

"Why did you keep it?"

"Because of the blood."

She thrusts the cloth into his hand, avoiding looking into his eyes.

Chamdi takes the cloth from her hands and sees three large drops of blood. It looks as though the blood has been preserved on the cloth especially for him.

"What's this blood?" he asks, surprised.

"I don't know, but I have thought about it a hundred times."

"Is this my blood?"

"No, you were clean."

"Is this my father's blood?"

"If that man was your father. That's why I kept it."

Chamdi listens to her breathe. It is as if he can suddenly hear every sound in the room, even the softest.

"Chamdi, how old are you now?" asks Mrs. Sadiq gently.

"Ten."

"You are no longer ten."

"What?"

"You are no longer ten. Age does not matter anymore. You are a man now, and it is my fault that I have made you the man you are. Forgive me."

Mrs. Sadiq leaves the room. Chamdi stands frozen, like a dumb animal.

He has thoughts, so many of them, that they do not resemble thoughts at all. Some are just words like *blood* and *running,* and he imagines himself as a white bundle near the well, a bundle that made a grown man run in fear.

THREE.

It is the middle of the night and all the children are sleeping. Chamdi is hungry and he regrets that he refused to eat dinner. But he did not feel like eating earlier.

He now knows he has to leave the orphanage before it leaves him. He rises from his bed and looks around. In the dimness of the small light bulb that hangs in a corner of the sleeping room, he tiptoes to the foyer, stepping on the children's rubber chappals, until he reaches the main door of the orphanage. He carefully slides the latch open so that no one else wakes up. The latch creaks a little, but he tells himself that on a night such as this a creak makes no difference at all.

He opens the door, steps into the night, and walks straight towards the row of bougainvilleas. In the dark, he cannot see colours. But he uses his mind to light the petals up, and after a moment he begins to see shades of pink and red. He likes this, how the colours stand apart from the darkness.

Then a horrible thought strikes. What if they tear apart the bougainvilleas when they break down the orphanage? He has loved them his whole life. No, he thinks, somehow they will survive. Buildings might come, but branches will break through the cement and continue to grow upwards, such is the power of bougainvillea.

Now he understands why he is watching the bougainvilleas in the darkness. He is saying goodbye. If he had to leave during the day, it would be too much for him. He thanks them for the colours they have given him, then rushes towards them and puts his mouth to the red papery petals, not caring if thorns prick him. They love me too, he thinks, as they rustle against his skin. They do not mind being woken from their sleep. He tells them he has one favour to ask. He will pluck a few petals to take with him, and he hopes that it will not hurt them too much. He stuffs his pockets.

There is one last thing he must do too.

Chamdi goes back into the orphanage. He does not need to pack, for he owns nothing at all. He has been given a white cloth with three drops of blood on it, and whether it bodes well or not, he will carry that cloth and nothing else. He ties it around his neck like a scarf. Then he takes a few red petals in his fist and walks down the short corridor into Mrs. Sadiq's office. She is asleep on the ground and he can hear her breathe lightly. He will not wake her up because there is nothing to be said. "Thank you" would be a stupid thing to say. In her heart, she must know that Chamdi is grateful for everything she has done.

He places a few petals on Mrs. Sadiq's desk and then changes his mind—he places them by her feet. Chamdi stands above her and thanks her with his mind and heart. He has never hugged her in his life and wishes he could do it now, but he does not want to wake her.

He runs into the corridor, out the main door and into the courtyard.

He does not stop to look back. He is not sure if he is crying and he does not care. He runs faster and faster. Soon he is only a few feet away from the walls of the orphanage, and he knows that he is entering another world.

If my father ran from me, then I will run after him. This is the thought in Chamdi's head as he runs. He is running because he knows that his father has had a head start. His father is miles and years ahead of him.

But there is another reason Chamdi is running. He is scared that if he walks, if he does not shoot through the narrow streets right now, Mrs. Sadiq might wake up and call him a traitor for deserting her and the children. So even though bits of glass from the street stick in his feet, he does not care. He runs faster and faster in order to catch the truck ahead of him.

The truck's heavy iron chain bangs against its dark green back. Chamdi has never chased a truck before, but he has seen other children do it. A white lotus is painted on the back of the truck underneath the words INDIA IS GREAT. He knows that if he jumps and falls, the concrete road will scrape his skin and break his bones, and it will not be the best way to start his new life, so he hangs on to the chain with all his might and uses the road to push off.

He has jumped into a garbage truck, and is surrounded by rotting food. As the truck takes a corner, a rat is jolted out of its meal, and it runs over Chamdi's chest. He tries to get up but then thinks that if the driver sees him, he might get angry and stop the truck. So Chamdi stays in the pile of garbage. The rat has gone back to its piece of mouldy bread. There is a crack in the side of the truck, more like a large hole, and Chamdi crawls towards it. The truck has gathered speed now, and the breeze blows bits of garbage out onto the street.

The city passes by, but Chamdi cannot see it in its entirety. He sees it in pieces, through the hole. He sees small shops, the steel shutters down, beggars sleeping under them. Stray dogs walk towards a tree and some of the dogs limp, but the others seem happy. A fair distance later, the road is dug up. A small fire burns in a brown drum as workers smoke beedis nearby, and a line of slum dwellers walk with buckets in their hands. So far, there is nothing out of the ordinary. There is no sign of the violence that Mrs. Sadiq spoke of and Chamdi is thankful for that.

As the truck takes another corner, Chamdi loses his balance once again and the garbage slides towards him. He lands on his back and is forced to stare at the sky. The sky is the same everywhere, he reassures himself. No matter how strange the city might look, or become, he can always look up at the sky and see something familiar. It is the same open space everywhere and it belongs to him as much as it does to anyone else in this world.

He feels he is quite a distance from the orphanage now. He wants to get off the truck, mainly to avoid the smell, but it would be foolish to attempt a landing at this speed. If it were daytime, the truck would be crawling through traffic. He is surprised at how empty the streets are at night. The truck goes over a bridge, and Chamdi can see tall chimneys around him, so tall that they must be friends with the clouds. Apartment buildings are so close to the bridge that he can see right into people's rooms—an old man is shaving himself in front of a mirror. Why is he doing that in the middle of the night? As the truck descends the bridge, the roads become narrower, and to his right, two policemen sit on stools outside a police chowki. One policeman has a beedi in his mouth while the other rests his chin on his elbow and seems to be dozing.

As the truck smokes its way through the streets, the policemen become smaller and smaller, until they are out of sight. A group of four or five black motorcycles overtakes the truck. Young men ride the motorcycles and their shirts balloon as they speed past the truck and swerve dangerously close to each other.

Then Chamdi hears music. It blares from loudspeakers, and he likes how even though it is night, a song is playing. The truck slows down. Maybe the driver wants to listen to the music. Chamdi takes his chance. He hoists himself over the side of the truck and lands on the street. But he is not used to jumping off a running truck, no matter how slow, and he loses his balance and falls backwards. He stays on the ground for a few seconds. Nothing is broken, he tells himself. Nothing is broken.

The building in front of him is lit up. It is an old building, only three floors, but all of them have red and green lights, tiny bulbs that flicker on and off, travel in a line and even change directions. Loudspeakers on the balcony spill the best Hindi music he has ever heard. He feels he has chosen the right place. Where there is music, there is happiness.

He sees a man lying on a cot with one arm covering his eyes. The cot makes Chamdi ask himself where he will sleep tonight. Perhaps some kind person will take him in and offer him a meal. He wipes the sweat off his face with his hand. The smell of the garbage has stayed with him.

The music stops. The lights on the building remain, although they no longer change direction. They look like green and red stars stuck on the building. He wishes the orphanage could have had lights like these. At least there would have been something to look at.

Chamdi is worried about getting food. He has not eaten all day. He missed dinner because he was in the prayer room and not hungry at all. He wonders what time it is, but then tells himself that it makes no difference. Ahead of him, a few people sit in a circle, on chairs and stools, and all of them are smoking. There are loud shouts once in a while, and the old man amongst them keeps coughing. Chamdi prefers not to go near them because he does not like the way they raise their heads each time they blow cigarette smoke, as if they have no respect for the sky at all.

An apartment window opens and a blue plastic bag slowly floats to the ground. It lands on an auto rickshaw. Chamdi notices that the rickshaw has no tires. It seems old and abandoned. Its rusted metal body is rooted into the ground so firmly that it looks as though the rickshaw has grown from the road itself.

A neat pile of cement tiles lay beside the auto rickshaw. The pile is quite high, and Chamdi sees two bodies asleep on the pile. They look like boys his age. It surprises him how comfortable they seem to be even though they are sleeping on a bed of stone.

The cough of a car engine makes Chamdi turn. On the main road, a taxi has stalled. The driver is pushing the car with one hand, and has the other hand through the window on the steering wheel. The passenger, a man, is straining to push the taxi from behind, while a woman sits in the back seat. Part of her green sari is trapped in the door.

Two of the men who were smoking notice the struggling taxi. They throw their cigarettes to the ground and walk towards the road. When they reach the taxi, the driver gets into the car and the two men push hard along with the passenger.

Chamdi tells himself that he would surely help too if he were strong enough, if he had eaten. He limps a little as he walks, and lifts the sole of his foot to see that it is bleeding. He remembers that as he ran from the orphanage, he stepped on bits of glass. He hops towards a patch of light that spills from one of the rooms in the building. He sits on the ground in that light and examines his sole. There are a few cuts, and he can see the glass. He carefully removes the first shard, then counts the remaining ones—there are four more to go, and he has all the time in the world, but he is tired and hungry. He tries not to think of food. The glass distracts him from his hunger, but he knows that the moment he finishes extracting every piece, the hunger will speak to him again.

He tells himself that he must be strong. He is ten years old, and he needs to find his father. It is a difficult task, so he will not let something as trivial as hunger discourage him.

The building looks different in the morning, without the blinking green and red lights. Chamdi can see the wires that join the tiny bulbs together and loop from one apartment to another. The gouges in the building are visible, as if it has been repeatedly pierced. A few wild plants have grown over the sewage pipes.

Chamdi has hardly slept all night. The hunger has not gone. To distract himself, he walks to a white wall that displays a movie poster—it shows a photograph of a police officer who wears black sunglasses and holds a gun by his face. The gun shines like it is the hero of the movie. There is also a sticker of a tiger on the wall.

He takes his eyes off the tiger and notices a tap attached to the wall. The tap makes a squeaky sound as he opens it, and the water that comes out of it is cool. He looks around to see if anyone is watching, but it is still early and most of the shops are not open yet. The street is quiet. He cups the water in his hand and drinks from his palm, but this process is too slow, so he bends lower, puts his mouth under the tap itself and swallows as much water as his body can hold. He stops only because he has drunk too much too fast and for a moment he pauses, watching a bullock cart on the main road as it carries a massive block of ice covered by sawdust. Then he drinks once again, and after he has had his fill, he puts his head under the tap and wets his hair, scrubs his face, and finally washes his feet by rubbing the sole of one foot over the instep of the other so that any glass pieces that are left will be washed away.

He decides to walk around his new neighbourhood. Soon he reaches the spot where the men were sitting in a circle the night before and smoking into the sky, and he sees a couple of wooden stools out in the street. A line of motorcycles is parked by the side of the street. He can see the abandoned auto rickshaw too. It looks even older in daylight and it has a huge dent on one side as though it has been in an accident.

On the main road, where the taxi had stalled at night, two tall coconut trees tower above the streetlights. They do not sway, because there is no wind. There is a bus stop as well, and a man leans against the foundations of the bus stop and wipes his brow with a handkerchief. Behind the bus stop, against the shutters of a closed shop, is a magazine vendor. He has hung his magazines on a rope, which is tied like a clothesline between two building pipes. Chamdi loves the manner in which the magazines fan out, as though they are about to fly away.

He faces the building once again. Even though the walls look old and tired, the apartment windows are colourful. Some of their frames are painted pink and the glass is blue. Clotheslines display red towels and green bedsheets. A small red bucket also hangs from a clothesline, and Chamdi thinks it strange that someone hangs a bucket.

On the ground floor of the building is a small mandir. Chamdi can tell it is a temple because even though the building is brown, this section is painted orange. Also, an old woman is selling garlands outside it. She sits on her haunches in a small stall and threads together beautiful marigolds and white lilies. When she finishes one garland, she hangs it from a nail on the roof of her stall. Chamdi wonders how many she will make. Eventually, a curtain of garlands will cover her and she will have to peer through them like a bride in order to talk to her customers. But the old woman does not look at him.

Ahead, there is a beedi shop. Chamdi tries not to stare at the packet of bread that is placed on one of the glass jars, or at the powdery biscuits inside the jars. He turns his head and walks faster, towards a doctor's dispensary. He can tell it is a dispensary from the red cross on the white board. He knows that the names on the board are names of diseases, which the doctor knows how to cure. He wonders if a doctor would list a disease that he cannot cure. I hope I never need any doctor, he thinks.

Chamdi feels it is important for him to observe his new neighbourhood. He knew each and every inch of the orphanage, after all. He walks back towards the temple and hopes that the person in charge of it is kind enough to give him something to eat.

But the door of the mandir is closed. It has an iron lock on it. He peers through the iron grilles of the window. This time the old woman who makes garlands watches him. She discards a marigold onto the ground. Chamdi is about to lunge for it, but it has fallen into sewage.

He peeps through the window of the mandir again to catch a glimpse of the god within, but there is not enough light. How can that idol be a god if it cannot provide something as simple as light? But he feels warm, so the god must have a warm heart at least.

A man hurries down the stairs of the mandir building holding a black file in his hands. His hair is oiled and parted to one side. The man looks at his wrist and rushes away, but Chamdi notices that he has no watch.

Once more the hunger talks to him. It tells him that he must find food quickly or he will become dizzy and nauseous. He is not used to

going without food because he is weak to begin
with, and even though he ate the same food every
single day at the orphanage, at least that food gave
him energy. The hunger tells him that although
his ribs stick out of his white vest, at least they
remain inside his body, but if he does not eat
today then his ribs will stick out even more, and
while he is sleeping they will pierce through his
flesh and show themselves to everyone, and his
new neighbourhood will be horrified by the sight
of *the boy whose ribs became tusks and left his body*.

So Chamdi breathes in deeply and walks
towards the beedi shop. When he reaches its
wooden counter, he studies the beediwala's face.
It is small and he has white stubble on his chin
and cheeks. He is almost as frail as Chamdi.
Chamdi wonders what excuse the beediwala has
for being this way when he owns a whole shop
full of sweets, breads, and cigarettes. But then it
occurs to him that maybe this is why the man is
so thin. Instead of eating, he must spend all his
time smoking.

"What do you want?" asks the beediwala.

"I . . . can you please give me something to
eat?"

"Do you have money?"

"No . . . I don't have money, but even a piece of bread will do."

"You don't have money?"

"No."

"But even a piece of bread will do?"

"I've not eaten since yesterday."

"Okay. Take what you want."

For a moment, Chamdi cannot believe his ears.

"Take what you want," the beediwala says again. "You want biscuits?"

Before Chamdi can respond, the man tries to open the lid of the glass jar that contains biscuits. He exerts some force, but the lid is stuck, and Chamdi hopes that the lid opens quickly before the man changes his mind. After a few seconds, the lid opens.

"Go ahead," says the man. "Take."

"How many can I take?" asks Chamdi.

"Take how many you want."

"I will take three, please," says Chamdi.

"Take, take."

Chamdi puts his hand inside the glass jar. The man slams the lid of the jar down on Chamdi's wrist.

Chamdi shrieks in pain.

"You little thief!" shouts the man. "First you steal from my shop and then you come to beg?"

Chamdi is confused, so the pain in his hand waits patiently.

"Yesterday one of you dogs stole oil from me! If you ever come near this shop again, I'll skin you alive!"

Chamdi sees the anger in the man's face, so he does not even defend himself. He simply runs away from the beediwala, past the temple, without even glancing at the god inside, until he stops near the water tap. His wrist hurts. His first day in the city, and he has been given hurtful words instead of encouragement. Maybe the cigarettes the man has smoked have damaged his heart, which is why he behaves in such a hurtful manner. Suddenly Chamdi feels very tired. He sits under the water tap and lets the water run over his head. The water has the coolness of rain.

The tap sputters and runs dry.

FOUR.

The sun burns Chamdi's neck and causes lines of sweat to trickle down his back. He wants to sit under the shade of a shop roof or tree, but he now understands that in order to eat, he must find work.

So he searches the stores around him to see if there is any place where he might work as a sweeper. He has seen Jyoti sweep the orphanage, and whenever she did not show up for work, he used to help Mrs. Sadiq clean up, so he knows what to do. He stands outside the New Café Shirin Restaurant: House of Mughlai, Punjabi, and Chinese Dishes. But the bald man who sits

behind the counter is screaming at the workers in his restaurant. It would be a bad time to
approach him.

The next shop, Pushpam Collections, an air-
conditioned clothing store, is out of the question
because he is afraid to enter it. His white vest is
ragged—it has a few holes in it and it has not been
washed in a week. Even the brown shorts he wears
have weak elastic.

As Chamdi hitches up his shorts, he notices an
old man read a sign on a blackboard placed out
on the street. The sign is written in Marathi, so
Chamdi does not understand the words, but he
notes the symbol of the tiger again. After reading the sign, the old man climbs up the steps to
the Pooja liquor store. The old man does not say
anything when he enters the store, but it seems
he must come here regularly because the moment
the shopkeeper sees him, he leaves the counter
and comes back with a bottle of liquor. The shopkeeper puts the bottle into a brown paper bag.
Does the old man hide the liquor in a bag because
he is ashamed of carrying the bottle openly? wonders Chamdi. The rows of bottles that are neatly
stacked in the display case remind Chamdi of
Raman. If Raman were to count the number of

bottles he has drunk in his whole life, they might add up to more than what this liquor store holds. There is a large grandfather clock in the liquor store, similar to the one at the orphanage. It says three o'clock. What time is it at the orphanage? The moment Chamdi thinks this, he feels stupid. He knows it is the same time in both places, but the orphanage seems to exist in a different land.

Near the Pooja liquor store is another shop, but its steel shutters are down. An old beggar has made his home outside this shop. He sleeps on a large gunny bag and a metal bowl near his head has a few coins in it. The sun hits the beggar hard in the face and the beggar squints back at the sun with equal force. Even though flies dot his cheeks, he does not seem to care. His eyes are open and he is trying to get up, but does not have the strength to do so. Chamdi wants to help him, but he is worried that if the old man is mad, he might hit Chamdi. He does not want to take a risk because he has already been accused of being a thief.

He walks back towards the water tap and past the mandir.

The window of the doctor's dispensary is covered with an iron grille. It looks like a big brown cage. Perhaps people break in at night and steal medicines. Chamdi feels sad for the doctor's patients. Whenever Chamdi has fever, he hates not being able to see the sky. The blue of the sky is the perfect medicine for burning eyes.

He wonders why the dispensary is not yet open. Perhaps the doctor is sick himself. That would be of no use at all. He remembers when Mrs. Sadiq used to get terrible coughs, and she would be forced to lie in bed for a few days. If any of the children were sick at the time, they had no one to comfort them.

Chamdi does not want to think about the orphanage, so he walks away from the dispensary. But as he does so, he feels dizzy. Suddenly he slumps to the ground. He hears a cycle ring loudly in his ear and he tries to get up, but he cannot. The cyclewala weaves around him just in time. "Blind dog!" he yells at Chamdi. Chamdi curses too, but he curses himself for being so frail, for not being man enough to last without food for even a day. It is the heat, he says to himself. He begs the sky for rain, but knows it is a useless request.

He can see the water tap in front of him. He must not pass out in the middle of the street. He must get to the water tap. He rests both hands on the road and thrusts himself up. The water tap spins in front of him. He reaches the tap and clings to it to gain balance.

Luckily, the water has started again. Just seeing it pour out gives him strength. He drinks as much water as he can and tells himself that his stomach is full. If he can convince his stomach that it is full, he will be able to stand. And he will not be lying to his stomach because it will truly be full of water.

But even though Chamdi's thirst is quenched, hunger makes him weak, and just as he did the night before, he sits under the water tap and closes his eyes to the sounds of the street. He has no idea how sound will help him, but since his eyes are closed, sound is all he has. At first he struggles because the street offers so many sounds at once. But as soon as he hears the ring of a cycle, he knows what he must do, he must use that sound to travel, he must allow the *tring-tring* to lift him, to take him wherever the ring has been, be it the hard streets of the city or the gravel of small pathways and alleys. And he feels himself rising, and his mind tells him that such a thing is not possible, but he tells his mind to go to hell, and the cycle ring gets dimmer and is replaced by a car horn that sounds like a rhinoceros in pain, yet it is powerful enough to take him away from the water tap and the movie poster above it, and he closes his eyes and smiles because now the car horn is replaced by a truck horn filled with the cries of ten rhinos and he knows that he will use these sounds to travel so far that even the policeman on the movie poster who is so used to chasing gangsters will not be able to catch him, and he tells himself that if he is lucky, his hunger will not be able to catch up either.

The red and green lights have been lowered. Without them, the building matches the sky dust for dust. It is a night without wind, so the shirts, pants, bedsheets, towels, and underwear that are left to dry on the clotheslines remain very still. The clotheslines sag with their weight. Chamdi misses the lights. He liked how they danced from one end of the building to the other. Black patches of tar form shapes on the building. He wonders how old the building is and if people who were born in it still live there. Is it possible to stay in one place your whole life? He thinks these things on purpose, to distract his mind from the hunger. This will be his second night without food.

He sits near the water tap and watches the main road. A taxi goes past, the driver's right arm outside the car, holding a cigarette, while he steers with his other hand. Chamdi hears the screech of a motorcycle as an old woman comes in speed's way, and the rider shouts at the old woman, who shouts back with equal venom.

A BEST double-decker bus slants its way across the main road. The white lights inside the bus are bright, and since it is late at night, the bus is nearly empty. A man with a long beard has fallen asleep with his head on the railing of the seat in front of him. Chamdi wonders if the man has missed his stop.

He takes off the white cloth that is tied around his neck and places it on the street, not caring if the cloth will get dirty. Apart from the three drops of blood, it is drenched in sweat anyway. He puts his head on the cloth and lies down. Each time his eyes close, his stomach opens them, administering dull pain to its own walls.

When he hears the sound of a truck, he recalls the garbage truck of less than twenty-four hours ago. He could have taken some bread from the orphanage. Mrs. Sadiq would have understood. All the children must be asleep right now. He has inhaled car fumes all day and he thinks of Pushpa, how she would not be able to breathe if she lived in the street.

Then Chamdi's eyes close on their own, without him forcing them shut, and images reel through his brain: the pigeons on the walls of the orphanage, bougainvillea petals leaning forward towards his face, and Jesus. He wonders if Jesus knows that he has left the orphanage. He did not get a chance to say goodbye. But over the next few days, when Chamdi does not show up for prayers, Jesus will realize that Chamdi is gone.

Chamdi feels something wet against his ear. He opens his eyes and sees a dog. It stands in front of him for a moment with a white cloth in its mouth, and then starts running, and on an empty stomach and with sleep in his eyes Chamdi must chase this dog because the only thing that connects him to his father is this piece of cloth.

Even though the dog is not fast, and Chamdi is usually a fast runner, he finds it hard to keep up with the animal. He can see it under a street-light, the hair on its back standing and shining as it turns a corner. The three drops of blood that might belong to his father give him strength, and he surges ahead, only to find that the dog is nowhere. Old buildings surround him, two-storey ones, and the dog could have entered any of the alleys—it is impossible to tell at night.

Chamdi bends over and spits out some bile. He makes a sound like a sick animal. He wipes his mouth with his hand and then wipes his hand on the front of his brown shorts. He hears a whimper. The dog stands near a huge garbage container behind a building. It still holds the white cloth between its teeth, but it is trying to climb onto the container, which is too tall for it. Chamdi creeps up behind the dog, but it senses his presence. He stretches his arms out, as wide as he can. The dog tightens its muscles as if it is about to pounce on him and Chamdi looks at how thin and dirty the dog is. He spots a blue plastic bag on the ground. It looks wet as though it contains something. He picks the plastic bag up and offers it to the dog. The dog does not move. Chamdi whistles softly and dangles the plastic bag close to the dog's mouth. Then he throws the bag high in the air. The dog jumps and drops the white cloth to the ground. Chamdi grabs the white cloth while the dog smells the dirty bag. He leaves the dog panting in the darkness, its tongue hanging out of its mouth.

I will never take this cloth off my neck until I find my father, he promises himself.

As he ties the cloth around his neck once again, Chamdi feels as though someone is watching him. He whips around only to see a rat entering a sewage pipe. If Dhondu the ghost-boy were here, he would insist a ghost was following Chamdi. Chamdi tightens the knot of the cloth around his neck and starts walking.

He comes across a barrel in the middle of the road. It is full of tar. If he had the strength, he would push it to one side. He ignores the barrel and hopes that no one bangs into it. He hears someone cough. It is a very heavy cough, one that can come only from a sick person. He looks to his left and sees a light on in an apartment. The cough immediately reminds him of Mrs. Sadiq, and he knows that she is not sick, but the loss of the orphanage has made her age so much in the past few weeks. He calls out to Jesus and says a quick prayer for Mrs. Sadiq, but the only response he gets is from the heroine of a Hindi movie as she stares at Chamdi from the poster. Her eyes are the size of moons.

Once again, Chamdi gets the feeling that someone is behind him, but he keeps looking at the poster and notices how, even in the darkness, the heroine's skin glows. He can read the name of the movie theatre—Dreamland. Large glass windows display posters and photographs of the movie that is playing. He goes and has a look: A man dressed in black rises from the flames of a truck explosion. A mother holds her child tight in her arms and stares angrily at a young man who points a gun at them. A police inspector is a few feet in the air on her motorcycle as she takes it over a jeep. Chamdi is surprised that the police inspector is a woman.

He hears footsteps behind him. He was right: someone is following him. He remembers what Mrs. Sadiq said about Bombay, that it is not safe anymore. But why would anyone harm him? Mrs. Sadiq was just scaring them because she did not want them to leave the orphanage and go out into the streets.

He spots a dangling lightbulb ahead. Steam rises towards the light. It is a food stand. There is an old man steaming something on an iron plate. The old man has no customers, so Chamdi walks towards him. Even though the smell has not yet reached Chamdi, his stomach turns fierce. The pace of his steps increases, and he reminds himself to have the right approach, to be polite and to ask for food.

Just as he nears the food stand, Chamdi hears a voice from behind him: "It's no use."

Chamdi turns around. It is a girl, about the same size as him. She wears a faded brown dress that is too large for her and her feet are bare. Orange plastic bangles circle her wrists, and her hair curls over her forehead as she leans her head to one side.

"It's no use," she repeats.

"Were you following me?" Chamdi asks.

It is quiet in the side street. Only the far-off car horn can be heard along with the wheezing of the engine as the car changes gears.

"That old man will not give you any food," says the girl.

"How did you know I wanted food?"

"Look at you. I've never seen anyone so thin in my life. You must not have eaten for weeks."

Chamdi wants to shoot back that it has not been that long since he ate. He wishes he were not so thin.

"Why were you following me?" he asks.

She looks him over thoroughly, inspects every inch of his body, and suddenly Chamdi feels very awkward, as though he is the only boy in the whole of Bombay. He wants water so that he can drink litres and litres of it and fill himself up to a giant size, but the water tap is far away.

"Come with me," says the girl.

"Where?"

She turns and starts walking. Chamdi does not know what to do. He wants food, and he looks at the food stand again and wonders if he should ask the old man to share a little of whatever is cooking.

"That old man is mean. He won't give you anything," says the girl. "But I will."

Chamdi believes her. He does not know why he feels this way, but he tells himself that so far no one has been kind to him. Perhaps his luck is about to change. So he follows her as she leads him through a narrow street between two buildings. Chamdi looks up at the sky. He knows there is a moon, but it is covered by the clouds. The inner walls of the buildings around him have a dark blue hue.

"Look down and walk," says the girl.

"Why?"

"You might step on someone."

Chamdi looks down and sees that people are
asleep under the open sky, and no one tosses and
turns. They must be at peace, he thinks. Or perhaps they are too afraid to move because they are
in the clutches of a nightmare.

Before he knows it, the girl has led him to the
main road once again. He is only a short distance
from the Pooja liquor store. As soon as he steps
on the footpath, headlights hit his face and he
loses his balance. The sudden shot of light in his
eyes reminds him of his empty stomach. He had
thought the eyes and stomach had no connection,
but he was wrong.

"Sit down," the girl says. "I'll come back."

But as soon as she turns to leave, a boy appears.
He is shirtless and his skin is very smooth. His
hair is short, cut right to the scalp. A deep scar
stretches all the way from his right lip to his ear.
Chamdi notices in horror that part of the boy's
right ear is missing. The boy must be two or three
years older than Chamdi. This boy is thin too, but
it looks as though the streets have made him tough.
His brown pants are rolled up to his ankles.

"Who's this?" asks the boy.

The girl whispers something in the boy's ear,
then walks away from them.

"Ah, yes," says the boy. "He's perfect. So thin."

"I'm not thin," says Chamdi sharply. But he feels stupid the moment he says this. Of course he is thin. The Koyba Boys at the orphanage used to call him a walking stick. But it did not upset Chamdi that much because in his dreams that same walking stick turned into a beating stick and thrashed the Koyba Boys to a pulp.

The boy puts his hand in his pocket and takes out a beedi. He lights it with a match, but does not throw the match away. He puts the used matchstick back in his pocket and blows smoke into the sky just as the men did the night before. Chamdi wonders why this boy smokes and why he puts his chin up and blows smoke upwards as if smoke had a choice about which way it travels.

"So you're hungry?" the boy asks.

"Yes," says Chamdi.

"But we have no food. We ate it all."

The boy inhales the beedi deeply, and as he pulls it away from his mouth, the end of the beedi makes his black eyes glow for a moment. His black eyes are narrow, unlike Chamdi's.

"So where are you from?" the boy asks.

"Here only." Chamdi decides not to tell the

boy the truth. He cannot show that he is new to the streets.

"Here only? Meaning . . ."

"I live on the road. Just like you."

The boy extends his beedi towards Chamdi.

"No," says Chamdi. "I don't smoke."

"You don't smoke? Are you a man or what?"

"I've stopped smoking."

"So where are you from?"

"I already told you. I live on this road only."

"Oh? What's this road called?"

"I call it by whatever name I like. What does a name matter?"

Chamdi does not like the way the boy smiles. He knows the boy is testing him.

"If you tell me the exact name of this road, I'll give you something to eat," says the boy.

"You told me you had no food."

"I lied."

He blows smoke once again. His beedi is half done.

"I'm waiting," says the boy.

"Kutta Gulley," says Chamdi.

"You know that's not the name."

"It's the name I have given it. Because this gulley is full of stray dogs."

"You're smart," says the boy. But he does not look at Chamdi. He looks at the beedi and watches it get shorter. "Can you run?" the boy asks.

"Anyone can run," says Chamdi.

"Not me," says the boy.

"Why not?"

"I'll show you."

The boy throws the beedi to the ground and uses his bare foot to stub it out. He then takes the used matchstick out of his pocket and puts it between his teeth. The moment he starts walking, Chamdi understands why the boy cannot run. His right leg is lifeless and it forces him to walk with a limp. He supports the leg with his right hand, and then he tries to run, and he does so with this ridiculous limp, and he smiles with pride as if he is a clown performing for Chamdi. After a few strides he takes the matchstick out of his mouth and asks, "How was that?" Chamdi wants to say it was wonderful, it truly was, but he decides he does not know this boy well enough to laugh at his deformity.

"Don't you ever smile?" asks the boy. "Or is your face like my leg? Without feeling?"

"I don't know you well," says Chamdi.

"But you just said we share the same address, no? So how come you don't know me?" He stares at Chamdi's body, just as the girl did.

"My name is Sumdi," the boy says. "And that was my sister, Guddi."

"Sumdi and Guddi."

"That's right."

"What happened to your leg?"

"So now you think you can ask me questions just because you know my name?"

"I thought . . ."

"Yaar, I'm playing with you. I'll tell you what happened to my leg. Polio. But what difference? It's only a name."

"Like Kutta Gulley," says Chamdi.

"Kutta Gulley!" shouts the boy. "I like that. So what's your name?"

Before Chamdi can answer, the girl appears again. She holds a steaming glass of chai in her hand. Chamdi can tell from the colour that the chai is very milky. She holds a slice of bread in her other hand, and even though the bread does not look fresh, Chamdi does not care. He gets up and grabs the piece of bread from her. He shoves it into his mouth and relishes the taste, but not for too long because his throat pulls the piece of bread inwards with great force and sends it to his stomach.

Next, he goes for the chai. His hand shakes as he raises the glass to his mouth. He blows on it a couple of times to cool it down, and takes his first sip. The chai tastes bland, but its warmth enters him readily. He wants to ask for some sugar, but reminds himself that he is not at the orphanage anymore.

Chamdi knows he is being studied by Sumdi, while Guddi stands behind her brother.

"He's perfect," says Sumdi again. "He's so thin."

"Let's hope he can run fast," says Guddi.

"I can run fast," says Chamdi, although he has no idea why he needs to prove himself.

"Show us," says Guddi.

"Now?"

"Yes," she says.

"I don't have the strength to run now," says Chamdi.

Chamdi does not like this talk about running. His father was known to be a runner too. He remembers Mrs. Sadiq's words, *The way he ran from you as if you were a ghost* . . . Or maybe she did not say that, but that is the sense he got from her, that he made

his father run. And now these two are asking if he
can run and it does not look like any good can come
of it. But at least they have soothed his stomach.

"Do you need a place to sleep?" asks Sumdi.

"Yes," says Chamdi.

"Ask him his name," says Guddi.

Chamdi does not like the fact that she does not
talk to him directly anymore. She does not even
look at him.

"What's your name?" asks Sumdi.

"Chamdi."

"Hah?"

"Chamdi."

"What a strange name. But I like it. You know
why I like it? It sounds like my name. Sumdi.
Sumdi and Chamdi. We'll make a good team."

Sumdi hobbles over to Chamdi and puts his
arm around him.

"We'll make a great team. I know it."

"I work alone," says Chamdi.

He has no idea what he means by this, but he
says it to prove to Sumdi that he is a man of the
streets. Guddi laughs.

"He talks like a Hindi movie," she says. "And
just look at that scarf he wears around his neck in
this heat. It was a bad idea for me to bring him."

"I will train him," says Sumdi. "Come with us, Chamdi. Our place is under a tree."

And Chamdi follows Sumdi because this is the most sensible thing Sumdi has said all night—that their place is under a tree. Chamdi notices that the tree in question is extremely still. Not a single leaf moves. The strange thing about this tree is that it seems to grow from the cement footpath itself. As he gets closer, he can see the earth around the roots of the tree. The tree must be very old, and the footpath has been built around it, he supposes. Attached to the trunk is a makeshift shelter of gunny bags, cardboard, and all sorts of materials that have been pieced together. A few bamboo sticks and ropes hold the gunny bags up. Chamdi can see two steel bowls, a packet of bread with four slices remaining, a rusty tin box, and a small kerosene stove. There is also an old wooden box with "Om" scratched on it.

"Welcome to our little kholi," says Sumdi.

Guddi lies on the ground under the shelter of the gunny bags. She scratches her toes and grimaces as she does this. Sumdi lies down on the footpath too. He crosses his arms behind his neck and stares at the sky.

Chamdi carefully copies Sumdi's actions. The problem is that Sumdi's eyes are now closed and it seems as though he will be fast asleep in a few minutes. Chamdi knows he will find it hard to sleep tonight. The orphanage offered him a bed and clean sheets. Here, the footpath is uneven, and stones and dirt poke his back. All he can do is stare at the sky and hope that its blackness will bring him sleep.

Then he asks himself if the sky is where his mother lives.

This thought has come to him before, but tonight he truly believes it. That is the only reason my father left me, he thinks. I reminded him of my mother. She lives in the sky now. Someday, she will show herself to me.

Chamdi stares into the darkness and traces the shape of his mother's body. From one star to the next he draws lines, connects them with skin and flesh. He picks the largest star to be his mother's head and attaches to it tresses of black hair, as he has always imagined she had. He does not use stars as her eyes because he has dreamt of his mother in the past and in his dreams he has seen her eyes: they are exactly like his, large and black, and he holds this image of his mother in the sky.

Soon his eyes close and he can hear Bombay breathe—car horns, the panting of dogs, and something else: the sound of a woman moaning.

Yes, it is quite clear to him that he can hear a woman moan.

He sits up on his elbows and sees a form on the floor, leaning against the wall of the building opposite him. It is too dark to tell who it is, but there is no doubt that the person is in pain. He glances at Sumdi and Guddi. Should he wake them?

If I wake them they might think I am scared, he tells himself.

But Chamdi cannot ignore the moaning. He gets up and slowly walks towards the person. He winces as he steps on something sharp and hopes it is not glass because there is enough glass in him already. He looks down—it is the red cork of a soda bottle. As he approaches the woman he notices that her eyes are closed and she leans her head against the wall. She talks to herself, but Chamdi cannot understand what she is saying.

Just as he is about to touch her shoulder to calm her, he freezes. There is a baby in her lap, only a few months old, and completely still. The woman's face is lined with dirt, and when Chamdi looks

closely, he finds that clumps of her hair are missing. She continues to moan with her eyes closed.

Chamdi is so close to the woman that he can
feel her breath upon him. There are creases near
her eyes and lines of age have been darkened
with sweat and dirt. Her mouth is dry and pale.
Chamdi looks at the naked child. He touches the
child's face with his forefinger. It does not move.
Go back to sleep, he tells himself. His shaking
finger pokes the child again, this time in the
belly. Nothing.

"What are you doing?" asks Sumdi.

Chamdi spins around.

"Don't be scared, it's only me."

"I'm not scared."

"What are you doing?"

"I was just . . . I think this baby is . . . not well."

Sumdi does not seem alarmed by the sight of
the woman or the baby in her lap. "Go back to
sleep," he says.

"But the baby's not breathing."

Sumdi puts his finger near the baby's mouth.
"I can feel its breath," he says. "It's sleeping.
Don't worry."

Sumdi then holds the woman's face in his
hands. "Amma," he says to her.

He gently shakes the woman's face a few times and she stops moaning.

"You know her?" asks Chamdi.

Sumdi puts his hand on Chamdi's shoulder and leads Chamdi towards their kholi. Chamdi wonders if Sumdi does this to support himself because of his afflicted leg, or if it is a sign of friendship.

"Go to sleep. We have work to do tomorrow," says Sumdi.

"What work?"

"I'll show you tomorrow."

They both lie down on the footpath again.

"Chamdi," says Sumdi.

"Say."

"You can run fast, no?"

"Why do you keep asking me that?"

"Just answer me. Please."

"Yes. I can run fast."

"Good," says Sumdi.

And Sumdi closes his eyes. His hand touches that of his sister, who is still sleeping, and she stirs in her sleep a little, but the touch does not wake her. And Chamdi's thoughts are still with the woman—he wonders why she is moaning and what she is talking to herself about so he raises his head and takes a look at her again. She bares her teeth to the moon and the child remains a statue in her lap.

Chamdi looks up at the sky once more and begs his mother to show herself, but maybe that is impossible, so he tells her to arrange the stars in such a way that the name of his father will be revealed, for if Chamdi is to find one man in this city of a thousand-thousand-thousand people, then the least the heavens can do is reveal his father's name.

FIVE.

The street comes to life early in the morning.
Crows sit in the trees and atop roofs and wake
Chamdi. He is surprised to find that a lot of
people sleep on the streets. A young man yawns
and stretches as he lies on a handcart. He sits
up, runs his fingers through his hair, and opens
his eyes wide. Two men pass him by with small
buckets of water in their hands. They smile at
each other as though one of them has cracked a
joke. A man dressed in khaki shorts uses a long
broom to sweep the garbage that has collected on
the footpath. An old woman sits on her haunches
and brushes her teeth with her fingers. There is

a thick black paste around her lips and she pours
water into her mouth from a blue-and-white-
striped mug and spits onto the street. She does
so in front of the sweeper and does not seem to
care that he has just cleaned that part of the footpath. A bald man in white robes walks barefoot
across the street. He holds a steel cup with a long
handle in one hand and carries loose marigolds
in the other. From the red tikka on his forehead,
Chamdi can tell that the man is on his way to
the temple.

Chamdi hears Guddi clear her throat. She
spits on the street too, just like the old woman.
Guddi's face looks dirtier than it did last night,
but her cheeks are surprisingly full. Chamdi
notices that she went to sleep with her orange
bangles on. The brown dress she wears has small
holes in it, and she wipes her hands on the dress,
uses it as a towel.

"Look at him," says Guddi. "He went to sleep
with his scarf on. I told you he's a complete idiot."

"Let him be," says Sumdi.

Sumdi must have been the first to rise, thinks
Chamdi. He seems wide awake. He opens a rusty
tin can and picks a matchbox from it. He lights
a fire on a small kerosene stove and places a steel

bowl on it. It is hard for Chamdi to take his eyes off the scar on Sumdi's face. It is deep and jagged, as though the skin had been torn apart. Chamdi wonders how Sumdi lost part of his right ear. If they sleep on the street, maybe a rat bit it off. Chamdi is grateful that this thought did not come to him last night. He tries not to stare at the ear.

"You want tea?" Sumdi asks.

"Will you stop feeding him and make him do some work?" shouts Guddi.

Chamdi looks inside the kholi and is surprised to find Amma there. She is mumbling to herself again, but she is not still like she was last night. She moves her body back and forth with the child in her lap. The child's belly is swollen.

"What's she doing here?" asks Chamdi.

"Why is that bothering you?" asks Guddi.

"I did not mean it badly," says Chamdi.

But he does not explain that he is surprised to see Amma in the kholi because it seemed as though Sumdi did not care much about her last night.

"Where can I go?" asks Chamdi instead. He directs his question at Sumdi and does not meet Guddi's eyes.

"For what?"

"You know," he says, awkwardly.

"But all you had last night was a slice of bread," says Guddi. She seems to have picked up Chamdi's meaning faster than her brother. "So were you lying to us about being hungry?"

"Pick your spot," says Sumdi. "Do it anywhere you want."

"What if someone sees me?"

"Ask them not to take a photo," says Guddi.

Sumdi and Guddi laugh. "And you expect us to believe that you have lived on the streets," says Sumdi.

"No, it's just that . . ."

"Come with me," says Sumdi.

He leads Chamdi about fifty feet away to three broken steps. One pillar stands in a corner with rusty iron rods sticking out of it. Slabs of stone are strewn all over the ground.

"This building got burnt," says Sumdi. "Only these three steps remain. And we got a bath-room out of that. Now crouch on these steps and let it land."

Sumdi limps away, and as Chamdi lowers his shorts, Sumdi turns and looks at him.

"Be careful of your jewels," he shouts. "The

rats might steal them." He slaps himself on the thigh and limps away.

Chamdi tries to finish quickly. Not that he believes Sumdi about the rats, but he is uncomfortable. He thinks of Mrs. Sadiq. If she were to see him in this position, she would be shocked. If the Koyba Boys were to see him relieving himself on the street, they would tell the world. He thinks of the toilets in the orphanage, and an afternoon two years ago when Mrs. Sadiq went to the market and Raman passed out in the toilet. When Chamdi bent down to wake him up, he could not believe how powerful the smell of alcohol was. He threw water on Raman's face and Raman got up suddenly and flailed his arms about and screamed. Chamdi ran out of there.

As Chamdi finishes, he does not know how he will wash himself. Still on his haunches, he looks around. If he were at the orphanage, he might have used a leaf. But the only tree in sight is the one sheltering the kholi, and the tree's leaves are too high anyway.

A round stone saves him. He spots it only a foot away, so he stretches his arm towards it. As he wipes himself with the stone, he thinks of the

Koyba Boys again. Maybe they should play koyba
with this stone.

He pulls his shorts up and walks back to the
tree. Sumdi and Guddi are already sipping their
tea. They share the same glass, pass it back and
forth.

"Did you empty your tank?" asks Sumdi.

"Yes," says Chamdi.

"Have some tea then."

"No, I'm okay."

"Maybe our tea is not good enough for the
raja," says Guddi.

"It's not that. I can see there's not enough
because you two are sharing."

"We're sharing the glass," says Sumdi. "We have
enough tea, but only one glass. So you also have."

He offers the glass to Chamdi. Chamdi hesi-
tates.

"Are you shy?" asks Sumdi. "Are you feeling
shy that her lips have touched the glass and if your
lips also touch the glass then . . ."

Guddi hits Sumdi on the wrist and mutters,
"Early in the morning . . ."

"Don't mind her," says Sumdi.

Chamdi watches as Guddi pours some milk
from an open vessel into the round cap of a bottle.

It looks like the cap of the liquor bottle Raman used to drink from. She then moves towards the baby, which is in Amma's lap, and pours a little milk into its mouth.

"What's she doing?" asks Chamdi.

"Feeding the baby."

"Why is Amma not feeding it herself?"

"Amma is sick."

"Oh . . ."

"She does not have any milk in her. Now stop asking questions."

Chamdi takes one more sip of tea and passes the glass to Sumdi, who pours some more tea from the bowl into the glass. Amma begins to moan again, and although she looks directly at her child, it seems that she is seeing right through it. Chamdi glances at Sumdi.

"She's our mother," says Sumdi abruptly, as he stares at the steaming bowl. "She wanders off with the child all the time. Now we are tired of worrying. She can hardly understand what we say to her. She just sits in a corner and tears her own hair off her head. I hate it when she does that."

"Where's your father?" asks Chamdi.

"Dead."

Chamdi wants to hit himself on the head for asking that question.

"You see that Irani bakery over there?" asks Sumdi.

Chamdi looks at the bakery opposite them. There is an advertisement for Pepsi above a board that says Rostamion Bakery and Stores. Below the board, a man with a large moustache dusts the glass display case in which the bread is stored. The first few buttons of his shirt are open to reveal a dense layer of black chest hair. Next to the bakery is Café Gustad, where a young boy sweeps the floor, stopping occasionally to wipe the sleep from his eyes. Black chairs are stacked on top of each other, and tables with marble tops and wooden legs are randomly placed throughout the café.

"A car crushed our father three years ago," continues Sumdi. "Just outside that Irani bakery."

If the father died three years ago, how can that be Amma's child? But Chamdi does not ask this question aloud. "I'm sorry" is all he says.

"What to do? There's nothing we can do," says Sumdi. "Our mother went mad after he died. And we have to look after her now. What to do?"

Chamdi feels awkward. Is he supposed to come up with an answer to Sumdi's question?

"You can help us," says Sumdi at last.

"Me?"

"We have a plan," says Sumdi.

"What plan?"

"To steal."

The thought of stealing appalls Chamdi. He has never stolen in his life. Not once. Even though he knew where Mrs. Sadiq kept the special cream biscuits at the orphanage, he did not take any except when they were offered to him.

"I'm not going to steal."

"Coward," says Guddi.

"Don't worry," says Sumdi. "It's a clever plan. Listen. Amma is very sick. If we don't take her to a doctor she will be finished. If something happens to her, who will look after the child?"

"Nothing will happen to her," says Guddi fiercely. "I will not let anything happen to Amma."

"You understand?" asks Sumdi. "We want to steal money to take her to the doctor and then we want to get out of this place."

"Forever," says Guddi.

"Where will you go?" asks Chamdi.

"To our village," says Guddi. "We have a village. So will you help us or no?"

She looks at Chamdi with her big brown eyes, and he is reminded of the kindness that he saw in them last night. But that kindness was so brief, he is confused.

"Why are you silent?" asks Sumdi. "If I could run, I would not ask for your help. Look at me, how can I run? If I run they will catch me and beat me till my skin peels off."

"But I can't run fast," says Chamdi.

"All this time you kept boasting that you could run fast," says Guddi. "So either you are a liar or you can run fast."

Chamdi knows he can run fast. When he was little, he heard a story from *Chandamama* about a boy who screamed so hard that he lost his voice, and then a djinn appeared and told the boy that if he ran fast enough he might be able to catch the voice. So Chamdi used to try doing this in the courtyard of the orphanage until he realized that it was impossible. But at least the story had made him fast on his feet.

"Please help us," begs Sumdi.

Guddi is about to speak, but at that moment the child in Amma's arms begins to cry. Amma moves back and forth, speaking—loudly this time—but she emits only strange painful sounds.

The child's cries mixed with the mother's slow wails make Chamdi uncomfortable. Sumdi rubs his temples as if a pain has developed there, and Guddi tries her best to calm the baby.

Chamdi cannot stop himself from staring at Amma. Her eyes roll upwards as though she is trying to look at the sky without raising her head. He believes that Amma hates the sound of car horns because it was a car that killed her husband. Maybe each time she hears a car horn, she feels something terrible is going to happen and it frightens her. He wishes Amma would say a word or two that might make her sound human, but all she does is howl.

Chamdi tells himself that he does not care if his father is poor, if he cleans toilets like Raman at the orphanage. All he wants is for his father to be in one piece. But there is one more thing. His father must remember that he has a son, unlike Amma, who has forgotten hers.

The sun has come out now and Chamdi stares at Amma's scalp. The parts where the hair has fallen out, or has been pulled out, are pink. He imagines her hands pulling out strands in clumps, doing all this work that her brain is not even aware of. He grimaces at the thought of this, then feels Guddi's gaze upon him. In the distance, he sees Sumdi perched on the three steps of the burnt building. He wonders if Sumdi also uses a stone to clean himself.

"So will you help us?" asks Guddi.

Chamdi knows that if he tells her he will not steal, she will call him a coward again, so he keeps quiet.

"We will steal puja money from the mandir. Are you listening?"

"Yes," says Chamdi. "The one around the corner?"

"Hah, that one. Ahead of it there's a doctor's dispensary."

"Why is there money in that mandir? It's so small."

"In two days they will do a puja for Lord Ganesha. There is a politician, Namdeo Girhe his name is. The story is that when his mother was carrying him, she was very poor. She had no place to stay. She used to sleep outside the door of the temple. People saw that she was going to have a child so they gave her money. She gave birth just outside the temple and the young priest in the temple told her that because her child was a son of the temple, blessed by Ganesha, her son would one day be a big man. And it's come true. So lots of people believe in this temple. Every year, on his birthday, Namdeo Girhe comes here to pray and places money near Ganesha's feet to make him happy. The money is collected in a plastic box and the priest lets the money remain there until night to show everyone how much Namdeo Girhe cares about God, and what a magical temple it is. That way more and more people come to the temple all year round and the priest gets fat."

"I can't steal God's money."

"We are his children. He won't mind."

"Why can't you do it?"

"I'm fatter than you."

"So?"

"Look," she says. "You know why I spoke to you? You're as thin as a stick."

"So what?"

"You'll have to slip in through the bars of the temple window."

"What?"

"Do you think the door is going to be open for you? We'll put oil all over your body so that you can slip in through the bars of the window. If you get caught, no one will be able to hold on to you because you'll be so slippery."

"Have you done this many times?"

"Never."

"Then how do you know all this?"

"My father . . . my father used to steal. He would talk with Amma and we would hear. It was his idea to rob the temple. But he died on the day of the puja only."

"I'm sorry," says Chamdi. "I cannot steal."

"Why not?"

"It's wrong."

"It's wrong? What about my father dying? And what about Amma going mad and not having any milk in her body to feed her own child? That's also wrong, no?"

"Yes . . ."

"Then it's right to steal. We just want to get out of here. We are doing nothing wrong. If my brother could run, we would not be asking you."

Guddi looks into Chamdi's eyes. A strange feeling wells up inside Chamdi, as though he has known her before. He tries to look away but he cannot. Guddi rubs her nose and the orange bangles she wears catch the morning sun. Everything seems perfect.

Except that she is asking him to steal. Mrs. Sadiq always warned all the children: *Remember, once a thief, always a thief.* She used to wave her hand back and forth as she said this and Chamdi is shocked to see Mrs. Sadiq's hand in front of him right now.

But he quickly realizes that it is Amma's hand and she is bringing something to her mouth. Guddi lets out a small "oh," and she reaches out to prevent Amma from eating, because Amma has found a clump of her own hair on the ground and has mistaken it for food.

Rather than look at Amma, Chamdi gazes up at the tree he slept under. It is as though this tree is afraid to reach far out into the sky, or perhaps its branches do not know the way to heaven. If only he could climb this tree, he might be able to catch a glimpse of the orphanage and talk to Jesus. He would ask if it is okay to steal to help someone.

"What are you looking up for?" asks Sumdi. "Waiting for food to fall from the sky?"

Chamdi smiles. It is strange being with this brother-sister. Even though he met them only last night, he feels as though he knows them better than most of the children at the orphanage. Apart from Pushpa, he did not feel close to any of the children. He wonders how Pushpa is. He feels guilty that he promised to read her the story of the Hunger Princess but he ran away instead. He hopes Mrs. Sadiq explains to Pushpa why he had to leave.

"Come with me," says Sumdi.

Chamdi follows Sumdi down the road. He spots a cow lazing on the footpath. A man walks past the cow carrying an air conditioner in his hand. The cow is in this man's way and he tries to shoo it away, but it does not budge.

"Where are we going?" asks Chamdi.

"To beg."

"To beg?"

"Maharaj, don't be so surprised. You are a man of the streets, no? So why is begging bad? It's the family business."

"I . . . but what do we do?"

"First, you tell me the truth."

"About what?"

"About where you are from. Otherwise I will beat you on the head with my polio leg."

Chamdi knows that there is no point in carrying on with his act. He needs Sumdi's help in a city like this. If they become friends, he can tell Sumdi about his plans to find his father. But what if they both laugh at him—especially her? But if a car had not crushed her father, if he was lost but living, she too would hope the way he does.

"Do I have to beg you to tell me?" asks Sumdi. "We must not beg from each other. The enemy is out there, sitting in taxis."

"I'm from an orphanage."

"What's that?"

"You don't know what an orphanage is?"

"Hah yaar, I don't know."

"An orphanage is where they keep children without parents."

"There's another name for such a place."

"What?"

"Bombay," says Sumdi. "You're smiling, but it's true. This city is our home and it looks after us. Very badly. Bombay is a whore."

Chamdi has never enjoyed strong language like this. The Koyba Boys spoke like that and he never found it helpful.

"What's the matter?" asks Sumdi. "You don't like me abusing Bombay?"

"No, I just . . ."

"Or you don't like swearing?"

"That."

"Few more days with me and you'll be shouting

gaalis like 'Pimp!' and 'Son of a Pimp!' from the rooftops. Anyway, at least you admitted that you're not from the road."

"How did you know?"

"So many clues. Just look at your teeth. All clean, in one line, so well mannered. That means you brush them."

"Yes."

"See *my* teeth."

Sumdi opens his mouth wide and Chamdi can see that his teeth are chipped and jagged, and they seem to grow on top of one another as if they are fighting for space. Chamdi turns away because Sumdi's breath is so strong.

"Not a single day I have brushed my teeth. But don't be fooled. They might be yellow and eaten up but I could snap your forearm into two if I wanted. Not that I would bite your forearm, but I would crack it if you challenged me."

"No, I believe you . . ."

"But more than your teeth, your style gave you away."

"My style of what?"

"You act like a prince. You think and then you speak. When I speak, the words just come out . . . like vomit."

As they walk and talk, a juicewala's cart catches Chamdi's eye. A plastic mixer containing orange juice rests on a glass case in which the oranges and mosambis are stored. Some of the oranges are arranged on top of the glass case. Chamdi marvels at the manner in which these oranges stay balanced in the shape of a pyramid, as if the juicewala is some sort of juggler or circus man. Chamdi would love to see the juicewala's cart at night. Surely the oranges and mosambis would shine brilliantly when the bulb in the glass case is switched on.

"Hope for a solid traffic jam," Sumdi tells Chamdi.

"Why a jam?"

"So that cars are stuck and we have more time at the signals. Do I have to explain everything to you? Can't you think for yourself?"

"But it's still morning."

"So?"

"So no traffic jam. In the orphanage we could hear the sound of cars only in the afternoon."

"What sort of place was this orphanage? What rubbish did they teach you there?"

"I learned how to read and write."

"You can read and write?"

"Yes."

"And are you proud of that?"

"Very proud."

"That's of no use at all, you fool! When you go to the taxis to beg, they are not going to ask you, 'Excuse me, can you spell your name, please?'"

"What do I do?"

"You must act like you are really suffering."

"But we are suffering."

"Hero, this is Bombay. No one cares about the truth. The people want emotion. Tears! Can you cry real tears?"

"On demand?"

"Yaar, I'm just playing with you."

Sumdi places his hand on Chamdi's shoulder, and Chamdi stops walking. In front of them, an old man opens the shutters to a small watch repair shop.

"Now listen," says Sumdi. "There should be no shame in begging. We are smart boys. If life had been good to us, we would not be begging. No one will give us work, so we have to do this. No shame in begging."

Chamdi notices that Sumdi's tone has suddenly changed. His voice is softer, but firmer.

"The tears will come anyway, trust me," Sumdi continues. "I think of my father and that car

going over him, and Amma screaming and running towards him . . . and I had to hold my sister
because I was more afraid than she was. Neither
of us went near the body. I think of Amma now,
how she sits in the darkness every night and pulls
out her hair, and even though I think about this
every day, the tears still come."

Then he spits onto his palm, greases his hair
with it, even though he hardly has any hair. In the
sunlight, the scar on his face seems even darker, as
though the skin has been removed inch by inch.

"Even with this face, I can still look chickna,"
says Sumdi. "Understand? You know how many
movie offers I get when I go begging? But I always
refuse. Who wants fame? Look around you—I can
pull my pants down and let it all go like a waterfall
anytime I want, and no one will stop me. How
many movie stars can do that?"

Chamdi still stares at the scar. He knows it
must make Sumdi uneasy. The edges of the ear
are jagged, like torn paper.

"I must look handsome for the aunties," continues Sumdi. "Fat aunties have lots of money."

With that, Sumdi steps off the sidewalk and
onto the main road. Chamdi watches his new
friend trail a black-and-yellow taxi as it slows

down for the red light. The taxi has no passenger. Chamdi notices that the buildings on this street are much taller than the ones near their kholi. TV antennas line the terraces of these buildings.

"Bhaiya, please give something," says Sumdi to the taxiwala.

"Don't eat my brains early in the morning," says the taxiwala.

"But if I have no food then naturally I will eat your brains, no?"

"Your tongue is sharp. Be careful or you will cut yourself."

"That's the problem. My tongue is so sharp that food is afraid to enter my mouth. Look how skinny I am."

"You don't look skinny to me."

"Look at what polio did to my leg."

"What other sickness do you have?"

"I'm in *love*. Biggest illness . . ."

"Hah!" says the taxiwala. He reaches into the pocket of his khaki shirt and takes out a one-rupee coin. He gives it to Sumdi.

"For one rupee what will I get?"

"You can get lost," says the driver. "I don't want to see your face again."

"Is next week okay?" asks Sumdi.

The taxiwala smiles. As the light turns green, Sumdi steps on the sidewalk again.

"That was very good," says Chamdi.

"Stop congratulating me and make some money."

"But I wanted to watch you first."

"You wanted to watch *me*? Me, who cannot read or write?"

"I want to learn properly how to beg."

"Then you are my student from this moment."

"Done."

"Show me some respect, you idiot. Call me Sir."

"Sir."

"Now pay attention. First rule, never beg from taxiwalas."

"But you just did."

Sumdi taps Chamdi on the head with his knuckles. "Don't argue with the master. You rarely get money from taxiwalas. But this one's a regular. I have known him for two years now. Every day he takes the same route. When he's in a good mood, he gives. With the taxiwalas you cannot use emotion because their lives are just as hellish as ours, a little better maybe. So they don't care about tears. And don't be stupid and tell them you can read and write because maybe they can't. You don't want to make them feel that you are cleverer than them. You are a beggar and beggars are meant to be brainless."

"Okay, I will be brainless."

"Sometimes it helps to act mentally disturbed. Especially with delicate ladies. Cross your eyes and make strange sounds. Bang your head against the taxi a few times. Go close to the window and cough into their faces. Guaranteed money maker."

"Right."

"Next are the lovebirds. You know what love-birds are?"

"I think so."

"Explain."

"Lovebirds are the . . . the boy-girl . . ."

"What are you shy of? Lovebirds are beautiful. That's what you must tell them. 'Look at you two, like Laila-Majnu, forever you will be together like two beautiful birds . . .'"

"May you have many-many children."

"No! Never mention children! The boy will slap you. He doesn't want his girl to become bloated like a football. If he wants a football, he'll buy one. No children. Just say that they are meant for each other and if you are lucky they will give you a coin. The best time to beg is when they are kissing. Keep on begging, keep on irritating, 'Please give money, please give money,' keep on saying it until the boy gets fed up and gives you a five-rupee note."

"Five rupees?"

"Yes, love costs. Now the biggest item. The foreigner. Man from other land. With these people you have to use pity. Make sure your face is very dirty. Put spit all over your face and underneath your eyes so it looks like you've been crying. Then go near the window and look directly into their eyes. It will be hard because they are always wearing sunglasses, but do it anyway. If they do not give money immediately, then say something like 'My father beats me,' 'My mother is dying,' 'My car is not working.'"

"'My car is not working'?"

"Say anything, it doesn't matter. They have no idea what you are saying. Most of them. But some of them are sharp and speak the language. Now there are many more types. But lessons for today are over, you may leave and go home."

"I'm already home. The streets are my home for now."

"Wah! What a line! You are ready. Now go and earn some money."

As Sumdi limps away from Chamdi, a van goes
past and blows smoke on Sumdi's face. Instead of
shielding himself from the black smoke, Sumdi
inhales deeply. Then he turns to Chamdi and
shouts, "Take it all in, it will make your lungs
strong!" He starts coughing. "Good way to get
tears," he says, "to let smoke go in your eyes. Dirty
your face, it's too clean. I wouldn't give you a single rupee! Stop walking like you own the world.
Carry the world's weight on your shoulders. In
a day or two you'll feel it anyway! And take that
white scarf off your neck. Bombay is not a hill station!" Then Sumdi laughs, and Chamdi feels it is
a strange sight indeed, to watch this boy walk with
a limp, a face black from smoke, and the widest
smile in the world.

Just as Chamdi is about to step off the footpath, a man on a wooden trolley rolls up next to
him. The man has no legs, and there is a deep
gouge above his right eye. Flies rest in that cavity.
He uses his arms to get off the trolley. He places
the trolley on the main road and then sits on it
again. A lump the size of a cricket ball protrudes
from the back of his neck. Chamdi turns away,
looks for Sumdi, but Sumdi is nowhere to be
seen. Instead, a small dark boy, not more than

four years old, stands on the footpath and glares at Chamdi. There is a steady stream of discharge from the boy's nose and he is completely naked but for a black thread around his waist. The boy does not take his eyes off Chamdi, so Chamdi is forced to close his own.

He imagines he is in the courtyard of the orphanage. A gentle breeze blows. The bougainvilleas sway towards him and he lets their petals caress his face. Soon they spread themselves all over the courtyard and climb over its black walls and into the narrow street that Chamdi passed through when he ran from the orphanage. The speed at which the bougainvilleas travel surprise Chamdi. They will be here soon, he tells himself.

A truck brushes past him, but he does not listen to the roar of its engine.

The car is a private one with tinted glasses. The thump of music emanates from it. As Chamdi approaches the car, he remembers Sumdi's instructions about tears, and tries to recall the first time he realized he was an orphan. But he cannot remember the exact moment. All he knows is that he was walking around the courtyard one day and Mrs. Sadiq was sitting on the parapet of the well, and when he looked at her, he suddenly understood that she was not his mother. Even though he felt a deep ache within himself that day, he did not cry. So that memory would fail to bring him to tears today.

Chamdi knocks on the window of the car and waits. The window stays up. Chamdi knocks again, harder. The young man rolls the window down, irritated.

"Get out," he says. "And if you touch my car once more, watch it."

Chamdi knows nothing will come of this. He walks to the next car, a taxi, and turns to look if the light is still red. A sudden gust of wind blows dust into his eyes and they begin to water. He rubs his eyes in vain and through a haze he tries to get back on the footpath. He almost bangs into a motorcycle. Then he hears the revving of the motorcycle's engine and realizes the light must have turned green. The cars have started to move. Horns blow. He hears the word "Chutia!" and the loud manner in which it is said makes him understand that the insult is directed at him. He blinks rapidly in an attempt to clear his eyes but instead collects more dust and snapshots of the grey buildings and the bending streetlights around him. His toe hits the curb and he yelps. He stumbles onto the sidewalk. Safe now, he sits on the ground and closes his eyes.

"Gaandu!" Sumdi's voice booms. "Why are you lazing around?"

"Something's in my eyes."

"Yes, your eyeballs. Now will you get up?"

"I can't see . . ."

"You are really delicate, yaar," he says as he hoists Chamdi up. "Now open your eyes."

"If I could open my eyes, there would be no problem, no?"

Sumdi pries open Chamdi's right eye with his fingers, his nails black with dirt. "Ah, there, I can see it." He blows into Chamdi's eye.

"What is it?"

"Dirt, what else?"

Sumdi keeps blowing, but to no avail. "Now don't move," he says. "I'm going to put my nail in your eye and remove the dirt, so just stay calm."

"What?"

"My little finger has a long nail for special purposes like when I need to satisfy an itch in my . . ." He stops deliberately. But Chamdi catches on.

"You're going to use that same nail in my eye?"

"Just a joke. Just a joke."

Sumdi delicately places his long nail in Chamdi's eye and flicks the particle of dirt out.

"Ah . . ." says Chamdi.

"Now for the other one."

But Chamdi opens his other eye on his own. The dirt seems to have disappeared. His eyes are red and watery.

"Perfect! Looks like you're crying. Now go and earn your first payment. Remember, Masterji is watching."

The light turns red again. This time, Chamdi is determined to prove that he can survive on the streets. He waits for the first few cars at the traffic light to come to a complete halt. He surveys each taxi. He spots a woman who is very plump and the heat has made her cheeks red. Sumdi's words ring in Chamdi's ears, "Fat aunties have lots of money." Chamdi wishes himself luck, puts on a smile in order to seem charming, and stands near the rear window. Just as he is about to beg and plead, he realizes that the woman is not alone in the taxi. A small boy, perhaps a year or two younger than Chamdi, sits by her side. He looks at Chamdi and says, "Mummy, a beggar." Chamdi's smile disappears. He did not expect to be faced with a boy

the same age as he. More than that, the boy did
not doubt for a second that Chamdi is a beggar.
Chamdi may be an orphan but he can read and
write—he is a temporary beggar. To be identified
as a beggar right away, in the manner a policeman or doctor would be, makes him lower his
head. Chamdi blames his dirty, ragged vest. The
boy in the taxi blurts out, "Look how thin he is."
Chamdi is still unable to look up. He wanted to
charm the fat aunty, earn money the way Sumdi
did with a tongue full of quick remarks. He tries
to suck his ribs in but knows that it is not possible. "Here, give him some money," he hears
the woman say. The next thing Chamdi knows,
he has stretched out his hand, and a coin lands
on his open palm. He does not look at its value.
He is still staring at his feet. He notices his right
toenail. It must have cracked when he hit his foot
on the curb only a few minutes ago. He clenches
his fist and turns away from the taxi.

SIX

On the footpath, an old man is dusting the glass display case of his clock-repair shop. He mutters to himself as he does this. Chamdi wonders if the man is muttering because all his clocks show a different time. Flies sit on the glass counter and the old man brings his duster down hard on it.

In the distance, Chamdi sees the skyscrapers. What would it be like to be on the twentieth floor of a building? Would he be able to view the orphanage from up there? Where he stands now, the buildings are only four or five floors tall. The children that live in the nearby buildings must have no room to play at all, he thinks. But they have the advantage of being able to fly kites from the terraces of their buildings.

Light falls hard on the sidewalk, which is busy and breathing. At a toy stall, orange and silver cars are placed in a row, and dolls hang in plastic cases from the roof. There is a plastic cricket bat, but it is very small, for children. Next to the cricket bat is a toy gun. Chamdi does not like the gun even though he knows it cannot be used to harm anyone. The shopkeeper sits on a stool and winds a two-headed puppet. When he lets go of the key, both the heads jiggle madly. The shopkeeper seems to enjoy playing with his own toys, even though people stroll past him and no one buys anything.

Next to the toy stall, a man garlands the entrance to his tailor shop. Chamdi wonders if the garland was made by the old woman who sits outside the temple. He misses his bougainvilleas. Why does no one make garlands out of bougainvillea petals? He has been without them for more than a day now and he can already feel the colour draining out of him. Perhaps he will be able to find a garden so he can recharge himself. With this thought, he remembers the petals in his pocket. He takes them out, holds them in his

palm. He notices a man passed out on the footpath. The man's shirt is muddy and wide open,
and black ants crawl around his toes. Chamdi
wishes the petals could make things better here
as they did in the courtyard of the orphanage.
But they do not. Perhaps it is because they are not
attached to the tree. He puts the petals back in
his pocket.

A moment later, Sumdi arrives and slaps him
on the back.

"They're all beggars," says Sumdi. "Those rich
people in the cars are the true beggars. Sixteen
rupees. That's all I made in four hours of begging. Today was a slow day."

But Chamdi is quite surprised with the amount
of money that Sumdi has made.

"What about you?" asks Sumdi. "How much
did you make?"

"I made four."

"I think the problem is your face. Your body
is very thin but your face looks healthy. Try and
look sick next time. Okay—we have twenty rupees
in total."

"So we can eat now."

"Not so fast, hero. We can't eat yet."

"Why not?"

·"First show me the money you made."

Chamdi dislikes the fact that Sumdi needs proof. But he reaches into his brown shorts and takes out a handful of coins. He opens his palm for Sumdi to see. There are four fifty-paise coins and two one-rupee coins.

Sumdi takes the money from Chamdi's palm and puts it in his pocket. "Right. Twenty in total," he says.

"Why didn't you believe me?"

"I believed you."

"Then why you needed to see?"

"This money does not belong to us."

"What?"

"It belongs to Anand Bhai."

"Who's Anand Bhai?"

"Anand Bhai is our boss. All beggars who work in this area must give him whatever we earn. Then he will give us some money back."

"Why should we give him our money?"

"Look at my face," says Sumdi.

"Hah?"

"Look—I know that since we met you have wondered about this ugly scar on my face and why my right ear is half-eaten."

"I . . ."

Chamdi finds it hard to look Sumdi in the eye. So he stares at Sumdi's shirt instead. It is cream in colour and has grease stains.

"This rip on my face was made by Anand Bhai," says Sumdi. "He calls it his signature. He cut me with a knife."

"He cut you?"

"After my father died, I cleaned tables and swept the floor in an Irani restaurant. One night as I was returning to the kholi, a man showed up and said he was my father's friend. He walked with me a short distance and then suddenly slapped me hard. I ran, but the fear made me forget that I have polio and I am unable to run so this man caught me easily and slashed my face with a knife. Then he said, 'I am Anand Bhai, and your father owed me money, so now you must work for me.' I was scared but angry and so I swore at him. That was when he sliced off part of my ear. So now you understand why this money is not ours?"

Chamdi looks up at the sky and knows he was completely wrong. A sky that overlooks such acts is not the same sky of his courtyard. It is not his sky at all.

"I did honest work back then," says Sumdi, angrily. "Now I'm a worthless beggar. I'm too old to beg, Chamdi. Only small children, lepers, and deformed people beg. Not boys like us. Other boys our age sell newspapers and magazines, or they become tea boys."

"Then why don't you do that?"

"With a face like mine, who will give me work? Even you stare at my face so much."

"I'm sorry, I . . ."

"It's okay. In any case, I'm not allowed to work. Sometimes I think I will have to spend the rest of my life working as Anand Bhai's eyes."

"Eyes?"

"A spy. I watch. I listen. Give him tips."

"Tips? What's that?"

"In a city like Bombay, information is everything. I stand outside tea stalls, jeweller's shops, at taxi stands, any place where conversations happen. And if I see something interesting, I report to Anand Bhai. You'll understand later."

Sumdi jingles the change in his pocket. "We need more money," he says. "We'll beg again in the evening."

Chamdi wants to ask Sumdi about Bombay— why Chamdi has seen no colours, no songs, no smiling faces, no exchanges of love. But he tells himself that he has hardly seen the city. He is bound to come across something that matches his imagined city.

"Can't we spend a little money?" he asks Sumdi.

"Not a paisa. I have to give Anand Bhai at least twenty rupees a day. No matter what. He doesn't need the money, but he'll do it to make me suffer, so that I remain his dog."

"But can't I spend my share at least? Anand Bhai doesn't even know I am here."

"By tonight, he will know."

"How?"

"Handsome will tell him."

"Handsome?"

"Did you notice a legless beggar with a hole above his eye and a big lump on his neck?"

"Yes . . ."

"That's Handsome. He begs in this area. He's also in charge of informing Anand Bhai about newcomers. So you are already registered, my friend."

Sumdi checks both his pockets again. He clicks his tongue. He grumbles to himself, and Chamdi can tell that the words he is spewing are abusive, but he has never heard them before. Sumdi is like one of the Koyba Boys. But then Chamdi quickly corrects himself. Sumdi's heart is clean.

The afternoon has proved to be a hot one, their palms are empty even though they made money, and Chamdi's stomach speaks again. Sumdi absentmindedly lifts his fingers to his mouth as if he is holding a beedi.

They pass a row of cycles, and shops that sell metal pipes and fixtures for toilets. Outside one shop, a man is hitting a piece of metal with an anvil. A little farther along is a cobbler, but this man has fallen asleep while sitting on his haunches with his chin in his hands.

Soon, Chamdi can see their tree. They are close. He feels ashamed that Amma and Guddi will remain hungry. They walk a little farther and come to a udipi restaurant. The woman at the counter talks on the phone in a language Chamdi does not understand. He loves the sound of this language. It is as though the woman is scolding someone, but there is no real anger in her voice. Her tone is playful, the kind of tone used on a friend who might have removed air from her cycle or tied up her ponytails.

Chamdi wonders how many languages exist in this world. One day he will create his own language. This thought makes him happy. He will invent words that are positive, that can only soothe, never hurt. But he asks himself if people on earth have the strength to speak with beauty. He will create a language that does not have the word "No" in it. Then his request for food will always have the desired outcome.

"Do you know the man who owns the bakery?" asks Chamdi.

"Muchhad?"

"Is that his name?"

"I call him that because he has a huge moustache. Why do you ask?"

"Maybe he will give us bread?"

"Hah! That miser did not give us anything even when my father died. He's a mean bastard who hits his own wife."

"How do you know?"

"He lives on top of the bakery. At night we can hear the beating and his wife crying. How can such a man give us bread?"

"Want me to try?"

"No use."

"There's no harm in trying." Chamdi is about to cross the road to the bakery, but Sumdi stops him.

"We have to try," says Chamdi. "Amma and your sister must be hungry."

"I never walk on that side of the road."

"Why not?"

"After my father died, we don't go near the bakery. Amma made us promise never to go there again. She said it was a place with bad luck. I think she was worried that something might happen to us. But see—she only went mad."

"Then why do you continue to live here?"

"Amma didn't want to leave. She would just stare at the road, and . . . my father's blood is still there. Somehow it has stuck on the road. It has refused to leave."

"We must try to get food," says Chamdi.

"Food is not the problem. There's a restaurant called Gopala a short distance from the tree. My father used to run small errands for the owner. Sometimes he gives us leftovers after lunchtime. Food is not the problem. We are not suffering from hunger."

"Then what?"

"The problem is that we live. We find just enough food to stay alive, and we are forced to live on and on in this hell."

As Sumdi says this, Chamdi spots the old beggar he saw the day before near the liquor store. The old beggar has changed locations

but the flies have followed him, and continue
to buzz around his face. The beggar's eyes are
closed, but he is talking to himself. Even Amma
talks to herself, thinks Chamdi. A city of so
many people and they cannot bring themselves
to talk to anyone else.

Chamdi's eyes are on the sweet breads displayed
in the bakery. He looks at the small room above
the bakery, at its tiny window, and feels sorry
for Muchhad's wife, who must spend her days
there like a trapped animal. Then Chamdi's eyes
move to a spot on the road. Although he cannot
see the blood, he feels that this is the exact spot
where Sumdi's father was run over by a car. He
tells himself that it is a good thing sound cannot
stain the road. It would be painful if the sound
of the car hitting Sumdi's father was stuck on the
road—and Amma's screams as well. People on
the street would be forced to hear those sounds
every morning.

Sumdi takes his cream shirt off and wipes his
sweaty chest with it. He uses the shirt to wipe
his underarms as well and then throws the shirt
inside the kholi. Sumdi is strong. He is not well

built, but his body has muscular lines and it seems as though these muscles are alive and breathing. Sumdi sits on the ground with his polio leg stiff in front of him.

"Take your vest off," he tells Chamdi. "It's hot."

"No, it's okay," says Chamdi.

"Be a man. Take it off."

Chamdi wants to take off his vest because he is indeed boiling, but he is ashamed of how his ribs stick out of his chest—even the boy in the taxi seemed appalled and gave Chamdi money. "No, I like it this way," he says.

"You like to have sweat dripping over your entire body? Were you a pig in your last life? Just take off the vest. Do it fast otherwise I will rip it off."

In one swift move that surprises even himself, Chamdi takes his vest off. No one has ever seen him bare chested, and now he has suddenly removed his vest on the footpath in front of people.

"Oh my God," exclaims Sumdi. "You're thinner than the temple bars! No problem you'll have entering."

"I told you, my ribs . . ."

"I'm teasing, yaar. You're too sensitive. In this city you have to be a harami."

"What's a harami?"

"A shameless bastard! Look at me, I have polio. Do I try and hide my leg or pretend that it's a walking stick?"

"How can you hide your leg?"

"That's another thing. You don't have any imagination."

"I do, I do."

"Prove it. Prove that you are not sensitive and that you have an imagination."

"If I do, then I get to keep the money I made from begging."

"Gambling already! You're learning fast."

"Okay, so here I am walking with my chest out. So it means I'm not sensitive."

"That means nothing. Do a little show."

"What type of show?"

"Watch."

Sumdi looks behind him, and sees two men on the other side of the tree, an old man and a young one, talking to each other and smoking. The young man holds the front of his white shirt with the tips of his fingers and blows onto his chest to cool himself.

"Look at me," Sumdi calls out to the two men. "I will give you a riddle. Whoever solves it will win a prize!"

The smoke drifting out of the old man's mouth bothers Chamdi. He feels sorry for the sky. Not only does it have to inhale smoke but it also has to look down upon a place that has beggars instead of flowers. It is a sky that has to hear the cries of Muchhad's wife.

The old man seems to be in a good mood, but the young man does not look amused. He clears this throat and lets out a glob of phlegm.

"How many legs do I have?" asks Sumdi.

The old man does not respond. He continues to puff smoke.

"What, you think it's simple?" taunts Sumdi.

"Two," answers the old man.

"Wrong!" shouts Sumdi. "I'll ask your friend. How many legs do I have?"

The young man does not answer. He motions Sumdi away.

"He's not in a good mood. Did his wife leave him? Did his girlfriend not like his lovemaking?"

"Get out of here before I slap your face," says the young man.

"You'll hit an innocent child who can't even walk? Are you a man or what?"

The old man laughs. His eyes are small and green, and Chamdi tells himself that this man must be from Nepal, like Kaichi at the orphanage.

"Okay, kaka, I will talk to you only," Sumdi addresses the old man again. "Last time I'm asking. How many legs do I have? Before you answer, I'll give you a hint. One leg is not working. Which is it?"

Sumdi takes a few clownish steps.

"Right leg," says the old man.

"Correct."

"Now which is the other leg?"

"Left leg."

"Now where is the most powerful leg? The hidden leg? The most important leg, your friend's leg which is probably *not* working, which is why he's in a bad mood?"

"Bhadwa, get the hell out of here," the young man says to Sumdi.

"Your middle leg is in trouble and you are calling me a pimp? Anyway, kaka, you did not guess, you do not get the prize. Now you have to pay."

"I'm not giving you any money," says the old man.

"Money? Is that all there is to give? What about *love*? Is no one a lover anymore? How about giving me some *love*? Or if you can't give love, then give me a cigarette, no?"

The old man reaches into the pocket of his grey shirt, takes out a cigarette, and throws it at Sumdi. Sumdi is unable to catch it. It falls to the ground. He picks it up and turns to Chamdi again.

"The work you need to do to get a cigarette," he mutters. "So you see? That's how you do it. Now your turn."

Chamdi is quiet.

"What are you thinking about?" says Sumdi.

"I . . . what's the answer to the riddle?"

"Hah?"

"What's the hidden leg?"

"Oh, you idiot. You unfortunate fool who spent his whole life in an orphanage, you poor boy, you know how to read and write but no one told you about your hidden leg. It shames me to share the same sun as you. But don't worry, tonight you will discover your third leg, and what a magical night it will be for you, chamat-kaar! You will never take your hand off your leg. But first, you have to complete your part of the bargain. Now put on a show for me, entertain me while I smoke so I feel like a king. Hurry up, do something."

"I will tell you a story," says Chamdi.

"I spit on stories!"

"*My* story."

"It will be a boring, well-mannered story. Forget it, just sit down next to me."

Sumdi looks for his box of matches. The cigarette is already in his mouth.

At first Chamdi wonders if he should pick a *Chandamama* story, but then he decides to invent his own story because it hurts him when Sumdi accuses him of having no imagination. Imagination is a private thing, but perhaps it is time to share his with his friend. Chamdi will tell his own story, but add and subtract a few minor details to make it worth a king's time.

"This is my story," Chamdi begins. "It is called 'The Boy Whose Ribs Became Tusks and Left His Body.'"

Sumdi almost drops his match.

Chamdi continues, "By the time you finish smoking that cigarette, the story will be over, and if you like it you'll have to give me the money that I made."

"I accept the challenge, you poor fool who has no knowledge of his third leg."

"There once lived a boy who was very thin. Whenever he ate, his imagination used up all the food because his mind was the strongest muscle, and he thought thoughts that no one else had the courage to think."

"Like what?"

"Once more you interrupt me I will turn your stiff leg into a hard whip that will give you a hundred lashes."

"Shabash!" shouts Sumdi. "I like you like this!"

"The boy dreamt of many things even though he was poor and had no parents. He dreamt of Bombay and how wonderful it was and how people help each other and do not fight or steal. Each time he saw something horrible on the road, some act of cruelty, his ribs would stick out more, and at first the boy did not understand this at all. Why are my ribs sticking out? he would ask himself. But one day his ribs spoke to him. His ribs said, *We are not ribs, we are tusks, and we are here to change the world.* And the boy told his ribs to shut up because what if someone were to notice his ribs talking? But he had no control over his ribs in the same way people seemed to have no control over their cruel actions. One day when the boy was walking on the road, he saw another boy who had polio. And that wasn't the only thing wrong with the boy. It seemed as if the polio boy had no brains at all because he was smoking too, but he was good at heart. And just then a horrible man called Anand Bhai came to this polio boy and took out a knife and said, 'Whatever money you make is mine,' and this brave polio boy tried to put up a fight, he fought like a tiger with one bad leg, but still Anand Bhai was winning, and then suddenly the boy of the ribs noticed that his ribs were starting to tear out of his body. They became sharp like elephant tusks and shot out through his chest but the boy felt no pain, and a tusk flew out and plunged itself in Anand Bhai's back and told him, *Leave this polio boy alone, he is a friend of the tusks.* And Anand Bhai ran away like a mad man with a tusk in his back. After that, all the horrible people were chased by tusks. Like that Muchhad who owns the bakery, a tusk came straight at him and smashed through the glass of his bakery and said, *Give bread to the beggars otherwise next time I will land in your throat.* And this continued until the bad people realized their mistakes. And then finally the tusks flew back into the owner-boy's body, satisfied that the people had changed."

Although Sumdi's cigarette is burnt almost all the way down, he has not taken a single puff. His mouth is slightly open and he stares at Chamdi.

But Chamdi is silent because he is catching his breath, and hoping that such a thing is possible, that his ribs can indeed become weapons that protect the good.

"Your cigarette is over," Chamdi says after a long pause.

"I . . . what?" Sumdi looks at his cigarette. "No, it's not over."

"I want my money."

"Where the hell did you come up with a story like that?"

"The mind can do anything."

"You are a champion. If you tell this story at night, it will be more deadly and I will feel as if a tusk is up my gand."

"Now give me my money."

"I can't, you beggar. The rule is, no matter what, we have to give Anand Bhai twenty rupees minimum. Per person."

"What if I don't make twenty?"

"It's your first day. It should be okay."

Chamdi wonders if Sumdi is inventing Anand Bhai. But Sumdi has been kind to him. He may want to steal, but he is not a liar. A liar is worse than a thief.

Chamdi looks at his ribs and the skin that

covers them, and how they gleam in the sun as though they are tusks. What if he is the biggest fool in the universe for inventing magic where none exists, in a city where he has only heard cries of pain and not a single cry of joy? Before he can answer his own question, Amma walks towards them from behind the rubble of the burnt building. The baby is in her arms. Guddi follows Amma, holding a small brown package in one hand, and by the stains on the brown paper Chamdi guesses that the bag contains food. In her other hand, Guddi holds the wooden box that Chamdi saw at night, the one with "Om" scratched on it.

"So did you make anything?" Guddi asks.

"Twenty in total," says Sumdi.

"I made fifteen," says the girl. "I sold one Laxmi and one Hanuman."

She places the brown paper package and the wooden box on the ground. The moment she opens the box, Chamdi cannot believe the colours that assault him. He feels he is back at the orphanage again, staring at the bougainvilleas. The box contains miniature gods, sculpted out of clay, painted in yellow, pink, red, blue, green, orange, and purple. There is Hanuman, the monkey god with his powerful legs and mace, Shiva with cobras twined in his matlocks, Ganesha with his elephant ears, and Krishna holding an imaginary flute. These are the ones Chamdi recognizes. He wonders why there is no Jesus.

"Did you make these?" he asks Guddi.

"No," says the girl. "An old woman makes them. I sell these for her. She gives me half."

"So you don't beg?"

"No. I work."

"Sumdi, why don't you also work?" he asks.

"I told you. I'm not allowed by Anand Bhai. You have to be allowed. And I do have a job. I am his eyes."

Amma enters the kholi, sits down, and lays the baby on the ground.

"What's in the bag?" asks Sumdi.

"Vada-pav," says Guddi.

"Aah!"

"A woman gave us some. I already ate."

"Is there enough for all?"

"One each. Amma has not eaten. I think the baby might die soon."

The matter-of-fact manner in which Guddi says this shocks Chamdi. He can feel his desire to eat leaving him.

"Why do you say that?" asks Sumdi.

"The lips have become all white like a ghost. Even Amma's lips."

"Let's eat," says Sumdi.

Chamdi picks up his white vest and puts it back on. Sumdi quietly takes the food from Guddi's hands and inspects it. Then he turns to look at Amma, who stares back at him as though Sumdi is not her son but a stone statue. Guddi lies down on the hot footpath. She closes her eyes and squints as the sun hits her face.

Sumdi offers Chamdi some food. Chamdi has lost his appetite now, but he takes the vada-pav anyway. The potato, placed between a single slab of bread, is still warm. There is green chutney as well and a generous dose of spicy red masala.

Sumdi quickly puts the whole vada-pav in his mouth, swallows it as fast as possible. Then he removes another vada-pav from the brown paper bag and crumples the bag and throws it away. He puts the vada-pav to Amma's lips, but Amma does not open her mouth. Instead, she slowly raises both her hands to accept the food like an offering. Sumdi places the vada-pav in her palms. Amma thrusts the vada-pav into the ground, and rubs it in dirt before raising it to her mouth.

SEVEN.

As night encroaches over the tree, Sumdi counts
the earnings of the day. Chamdi and he begged
all evening. Sumdi now has twenty-five rupees of
his own. Chamdi has only seven. Still, they cannot
buy anything with the money. Anand Bhai must be
given the entire amount. He will take his share and
hand over whatever money remains. More impor-
tantly, Chamdi must be introduced to Anand
Bhai, for if Anand Bhai finds out that someone
new is begging in his area without permission, he
might cut off a thumb or toe.

Chamdi watches Sumdi walk over to the burnt
building to relieve himself. Although Chamdi is

now alone with Guddi, Guddi does not even look his way. He wants to ask her where Amma is, but decides against it. He thinks about what he would do if Amma were his mother. He would never let go of her, no matter if she were mad.

He sniffs the white cloth that is around his neck. It smells more of himself than of his father. He cannot understand how this small piece of fabric once held his entire body.

"Stop playing with your scarf," says Guddi. "Why do you wear that stupid scarf around your neck in this heat?" She holds a tin can in her hand, looks into it—it probably contains a little money. "The puja is tomorrow," she says, looking Chamdi's way at last.

"Tomorrow?"

"So don't eat anything until then."

"Why not?"

"Don't put on any weight. You need to be thin enough to slip through the bars."

"I'm not going to steal. I did not say yes to robbing the temple."

"Then why are you still here? Get out."

Chamdi is struck by Guddi's harsh words. He hates that she takes for granted that he will steal. But then why *is* he still with Sumdi and Guddi?

He should leave. His real job is to find his father. He notices that the cloth around his neck is damp with sweat. If only a gust of wind would whisk that cloth off his neck and take it far into the sky. Over chimneys and tall buildings it would float, and he would make good use of his fast feet by following the cloth. When it would land and touch his father's feet, Chamdi would do the same. But instead of a strong wind, he gets Guddi's words: "I saw your ribs this afternoon. They might get you stuck between the bars. Learn to pull them in."

"I don't want to," he answers.

"Do as I say and you'll be happy," she orders. "Suck your stomach in. Pull your chest in and hold your breath for as long as you can. Practise from this moment on until the time you come out of that temple with the money."

Chamdi looks at her: a little girl in a brown dress that is too large for her, orange bangles on her wrists, dark circles under her brown eyes. He notes the way her sunburnt hair curls, covers her right eye, and how, even though it is night, she stands apart from the rest of the scene. It is only natural, he says to himself, that she stands apart because she is surrounded by a burnt building and small, dimly lit shops. But even if she were to stand in the middle of a forest, she would still stand apart, just like a ferocious baby tigress would in the middle of wind and grass and swaying trees.

"What are you staring at?" she asks.

"I . . . nothing. I was listening to you."

"Even after I stopped talking?"

Just in time, Sumdi appears. His eyebrows are wet. Chamdi thinks, approvingly, that he must have just washed his face. Perhaps Sumdi uses the same water tap that Chamdi does.

"Are we ready?" Sumdi asks.

"For what?" asks Chamdi.

"Our visit to Anand Bhai."

"*Our* visit?"

"You're the newcomer. You must meet him. If you don't, parts of your body will mysteriously start disappearing."

"As it is he has so little," murmurs Guddi.

"Ah, so the two of you have become friends," says Sumdi. "Guddi, do you know that he can read and write?"

Guddi's eyes widen, but she says nothing. She hides the tin can she has been holding in a hole in the ground and places a thick slab of stone over it. "Let's go," she says.

"She's also coming?" whispers Chamdi to Sumdi. "Isn't it dangerous?"

"What are you whispering?" Guddi asks.

"He's saying what an angel you are," says Sumdi.

"Especially when she speaks," says Chamdi, loud enough for Guddi to hear.

"If you don't like the way I speak, cover your ears," she says. "Or better still, ask Anand Bhai to cut them off."

"She doesn't mean it," says Sumdi. "She's in love with you, that's all. She saw your ribs this afternoon and it has made her so passionate that all these love-words are coming out of her mouth."

"Just be quiet," says Chamdi to Sumdi. "Can you do that for the rest of the walk?"

"Walk?" says Guddi. "You think we're going for a walk? Oh we're going for a walk to Anand Bhai's adda and on the way we'll see pretty flowers . . ."

"Guddi, he's new to this," says Sumdi. "Now let's be quiet otherwise our little thief will throw a fit and leave for good."

Remember, once a thief, always a thief. Chamdi wishes Mrs. Sadiq's words would not keep ringing in his ears.

The three of them walk past the burnt building and approach a grey wall. There is a hole in the wall, large enough for them to slip through. On the other side is a school playground, a small one. As they cross the playground, Chamdi sees three holes in the gravel. Perhaps cricket stumps were hammered into the ground here, he thinks. The thought of cricket energizes him. He knows he does not have the height to be a fast bowler, nor the strength to lift a heavy bat and hit the ball out of a stadium, but he can run fast. He will be the world's best fielder. If the opposing batsman sends the ball crashing towards the boundary line, Chamdi will run and dive, he will do anything necessary to stop the ball. Then he will throw the ball back to the wicket keeper with such force that the whole stadium will erupt. With the applause ringing in his ears, he walks across the school playground.

The three of them reach another wall that marks the end of the school property. There is no hole in the wall this time. Instead, there is a small iron gate. A stray dog lies next to the gate, asleep on its side. It breathes heavily. There is saliva around its mouth and fallen leaves on its body. As they approach, the dog opens an eye, then closes it and goes back to sleep. Guddi bends down, rubs the dog's stomach, and says, "My Moti is not well." Chamdi watches her move her face closer to its head, as if she is talking to the dog, but he cannot hear what she is saying. She dusts the leaves off the dog's body, places her palm on the dog's forehead, and closes her eyes for a few seconds. Then she walks through the gate into a square.

In the darkness, Chamdi can see a few human shapes illuminated in the windows that overlook the square, sitting in what appear to be one-room homes. The smell of beedis is overpowering, there is the loud cry of an infant, and a goat is tied to a small wooden post in a far corner. The area is unusually calm—it makes him uneasy.

"Is this it?" asks Chamdi.

"Yes," says Sumdi.

"Where's Anand Bhai?"

"Underground," whispers Guddi. "The ground will open up and he will rise like a bhoot."

"Stop fooling. Anand Bhai has sharp ears," says Sumdi. "Chamdi, do you see that goat there?"

"Yes," answers Chamdi.

"That's Anand Bhai."

Brother and sister try hard to stifle their laughter. An old man totters past, smoking a beedi. He points his fingers towards Sumdi and is about to say something when he is seized by a coughing fit. He holds his chest as he coughs, but makes sure he does not drop the beedi. When he has stopped coughing, he spits in their direction and walks off to where the goat is. He sits on the ground next to the goat.

"That old man hated my father," says Sumdi.

"Why?" asks Chamdi.

"Because the old man tried to touch our Amma. Amma was pretty at one time, you know."

It is hard for Chamdi to think of Amma as pretty. All he can picture is her scalp.

"My father did not like anyone looking at Amma," continues Sumdi, "so when this old man tried to touch her, my father beat the hell out of him. I will do that to Anand Bhai someday."

"No, you won't," says Guddi. "We won't be in Bombay anymore."

"I'll come back for him," shoots Sumdi.

The three of them stand in silence. Chamdi watches the light of the old man's beedi get sharper and sharper as he sucks on the beedi.

"Now be careful what you say," warns Sumdi. "Anand Bhai will show up any moment."

"Look, there's Chottu and Munna," says Guddi.

Two boys approach them. They carry something in their hands, but Chamdi cannot make out what it is. These two boys do not look like beggars. They are dressed in blue jeans and shirts and plastic sandals.

"Who are they?" asks Chamdi. He feels envious when he sees how clean their clothes are.

"The fat one is Munna. He sells newspapers," answers Sumdi. "The thin one, Chottu, is blind. He sells movie magazines. But they are both trained thieves. We all collect here at night. This place will fill up in no time."

And true to his word, four other boys appear. Chamdi has not seen such deformity before, and to see it all in one place is too much for him. So he tries not to look at the boys who are much younger than him, one of whom is without an arm, one whose nose is eaten up.

Handsome appears as well. Chamdi tries to get rid of the image of flies filling the deep gash above Handsome's eye.

The air is still. The baby's cries have subsided. From the corner where the goat stands comes a legless boy who wears slippers on his palms and sits on a wooden trolley. A rope is tied to his waist. A girl, maybe a couple of years older than him, tugs the rope, carts him forward. From time to time, the boy places his slipper-palms on the ground and gives himself a hard push.

"That boy's name is Jackpot," whispers Sumdi.

"Jackpot?" It is the first time Chamdi has heard the word.

"It means he's lucky. He's only four years old so foreigners give him lots of money. He begs at Colaba, a rich area. Anand Bhai is so fond of him that Jackpot is allowed to take a taxi from here to the begging spot and back."

Chamdi stares at Jackpot. How did he lose his legs? It is cruel to call someone lucky because they are without legs. Even Handsome has a name that does not match his appearance. No one will be deformed in Kahunsha, Chamdi decides. He clenches his fist tight as though his dream city is in the palm of his hand.

Soon they are all huddled in a group. Chamdi stares at Chottu, the blind boy with silver eyes. Chottu faces everyone at an angle, with one ear forward. Even Sumdi stands at an angle, as though he is hard of hearing.

The old man who was sitting near the goat now comes towards them, this time with a cane basket in his hand. He throws the basket onto the ground and walks away. Someone tosses a pair of ladies' slippers into the basket. They look new. A man's watch lands in the basket as well. A set of keys. Then men's underwear, brand new, is added to the pile. "Who got that?" someone asks. And someone answers, "It's your father's. After his balls were cut off, he had no use for them." Everyone laughs. Someone drops a bulging wallet into the basket.

Chamdi notices the silhouette of a man who stands in the half-light of one of the small rooms. Both his arms are above his head, holding on to the low roof. His body is arched forward. He steps off the landing and strides towards them, buttoning up his white shirt, running his fingers through his hair. As he comes closer, Chamdi notices that the man's eyes, though a piercing black, seem bloodshot, and have dark circles underneath them.

Sumdi nudges Chamdi with his elbow. This must be Anand Bhai.

Anand Bhai peers down into the cane basket and rubs his thick beard. There are beads of perspiration around his neck and under his eyes. He pushes his unruly black hair off his forehead.

"Who got the wallet?" he asks.

The blind boy raises his hand.

"Tell us how, Chottu. Maybe these other pimps can learn," says Anand Bhai.

"I found it. That's all."

"Hah?"

"It was on the ground. I had gone for a shit just behind Khalid's video library, and I stepped on it. Someone must have dropped it."

"And here I thought this was the result of years of training. Blind as a truck driver and you find a wallet." Anand Bhai laughs, and the others join in. But Chamdi notes that everyone remains alert, as if they might stop at the slightest command to do so.

"The keys. Who got the keys?" continues Anand Bhai.

"They are car keys," says Munna.

Munna sells newspapers, thinks Chamdi. And the blind one is Chottu. He sells movie magazines. Chamdi suddenly realizes that he is making a mental note of their names and jobs. He stops immediately.

"These are the keys to a white 118 NE," says Munna, beaming. "Outside Mohan Sarees. I took it from old Mohan's pocket after he locked the car and the shop. He parks the car there only because he lives above the shop. I dropped my newspapers right on his feet so he got irritated and started shouting. It was easy because he was angry. Anyway, someone can go pick the car up now. Mohan won't realize until morning."

"Very good, Munna," says Anand Bhai. "Now, which idiot got men's underwear?"

"That was also me," says Munna. "Because after you steal Mohan's car, he'll be poor and naked, and we'll send him this underwear just for fun."

"Next time, don't risk stealing underwear."

"Yes, Anand Bhai."

"Ladies' slippers, hah. I'll give this to Rani. Munna, go give this to Rani. She's in my room. Go in quietly because she's naked on the bed. First see all you want and then knock on the door. Your prize since you got a car for me."

"Thank you, Anand Bhai."

"Even I want to go," says Chottu.

"But you're blind."

"I'll smell."

"Hah! You dog! Maybe next time."

"But I got a wallet."

"I said next time."

"Yes, Anand Bhai."

Munna waddles along. Chamdi asks himself if such a clumsy person can be a good thief.

"Run!" shouts Anand Bhai. "Run before she wears her clothes." As Munna runs, Anand Bhai rubs his beard: "Running after whores at such a young age. Very sad."

Just as Anand Bhai is about to turn his attention back to the rest of the group, something falls out of Munna's shirt and lands on the gravel. Munna does not look at the ground—he looks straight at Anand Bhai.

"What's that?" asks Anand Bhai.

Munna stands perfectly still. He does not answer. Only the goat's bleating can be heard. Chamdi tries to discern what has fallen on the ground but cannot tell. The light that spills from Anand Bhai's room falls a few feet short of it.

"I asked you what it is," says Anand Bhai.

"Nothing, I just . . ."

"Bring it here."

Munna picks up the object and brings it to Anand Bhai. "It's a knife," he says proudly as he hands it to Anand Bhai. His manner of speaking is now extra casual.

The knife is inside some sort of leather casing. Anand Bhai slides it out. "It's huge," he says.

"Butcher's knife."

"Stolen?"

"Yes, the butcher went up a building to deliver meat and he left his cycle down and I found this in his bag. It's really huge, so I took it."

"So you took it, hah?"

"Yes, it's good to carry a knife."

"So when were you going to give it to me?"

"I was saving it. I wanted to give it to you as a birthday present."

Anand Bhai slaps Munna hard across the face. Munna rocks back, but does not fall to the ground. Anand Bhai is calm. He does not look at Munna, but feels the blade of the knife with the tips of his fingers.

"I've told you all many times, no weapons. If any policewala sees, then we have to pay him. Many times I've told you pimps."

"Who cares about the police?" asks Munna.

In one swift motion, Anand Bhai slashes Munna across the right eye. Blood spurts out. The ladies' slippers that were in Munna's hand fall to the floor. Then Munna is painfully silent as he bends over and covers his eye. No one looks directly at him. Chottu grits his teeth. He may be blind but he seems to be aware that something terrible has happened. One low, raspy "aah" from Munna joins the bleating of the goat.

"Take him to Darzi," says Anand Bhai, to no one in particular.

He wipes the blood off the knife with his white shirt. Chottu leads Munna away, to the room on their left. A young man opens the door. He sees Munna and then looks at Anand Bhai.

"Navin, ask Darzi to take care of this one," says Anand Bhai.

"What happened?" asks Navin. He is thin and wipes the sleep from his eyes.

"Munna thinks he's a big don. Take care of him, brother."

Chamdi wonders if that is truly Anand Bhai's brother or if it is just a manner of speaking. The young man does not resemble Anand Bhai at all. He is clean-shaven and very thin.

"Okay, Anand," replies Navin.

They must be brothers, thinks Chamdi. No one has called Anand Bhai by his first name. Navin lets Munna and Chottu in and closes the door.

"I have something important to tell you all," Anand Bhai says. "There was an incident in the city last night. Does anyone know where Radhabai Chawl is?"

No one answers.

"Radhabai Chawl is in Jogeshwari," continues Anand Bhai. "A Hindu family was sleeping in their room. Six people in all. Some say there were nine of them. We are not sure at this point. But the family included two children and one crippled girl. Some men bolted the door from outside and threw a petrol bomb in from the window. The family was burnt alive. Some say only the cripple girl survived."

Anand Bhai purses his lips. Then he sticks his tongue between his teeth as if something is stuck in there.

"Do you know who did this?" he asks.

In the silence that follows Anand Bhai's question, Chamdi thinks of Mrs. Sadiq. Perhaps she was right. Bombay has gone mad and people are hurting each other in terrifying ways.

"I'll give you a hint," says Anand Bhai. "The neighbours heard shouts of 'Allah-O-Akbar' as the flames were rising. So let me ask you again: Who did this?"

"Muslims," comes the answer.

"Yes. Muslims," says Anand Bhai.

"Why did they burn them?" asks Jackpot, the boy without legs. Chamdi is surprised when he hears Jackpot's voice. It is truly the soft voice of a child. Jackpot raises one hand to his face, but realizes that his slipper is on his hand, so he puts his hand back on the ground, takes the slipper off, and then scratches his nose.

"They burnt them because of Babri Masjid," replies Anand Bhai.

The name is familiar to Chamdi. The Hindus broke down the Babri Masjid, a mosque in Ayodhya, a faraway place, Mrs. Sadiq had said, and now Hindus and Muslims were hurting each other in Bombay because of that.

A few days later, when Raman was cleaning the toilets, Chamdi had asked why the Hindus broke down the mosque. Raman explained that Ayodhya was where Lord Rama was born. Hundreds of years ago, there used to be a temple there. A Mughal ruler called Babur broke down the Ram temple and built the Babri Masjid in its place. Now the Hindus want that temple rebuilt. So they destroyed the mosque. At the time, Chamdi dismissed Raman's words as those of a drunkard.

As Chamdi recalls this, Anand Bhai calmly removes a packet of Gold Flake cigarettes from the pocket of his white shirt. He takes out a cigarette and puts it into his mouth. He holds the cigarette very lightly between his lips, and Chamdi feels the cigarette will fall to the ground at any moment. Anand Bhai then uses a gold lighter and speaks with the burning cigarette in his mouth.

"This retaliation from Muslims should not have happened. Mark my words, the flames of Radhabai Chawl will spread all over Bombay," he says. "The order has come from very high. There will be more riots. Killing, raping."

Chamdi takes a step back when he hears Anand Bhai talk about killing. Sumdi firmly holds Chamdi's shoulders and Chamdi understands that he must stay calm and not move again.

"I have organized a group of men," says Anand Bhai. "You boys must also join in. It will be good training. Get ready to bajao some young Muslim girls. Shops will be looted also. Police will be on our side, no fear."

Chamdi feels uneasy. He did not understand all of what Anand Bhai just said. But the word *killing* is known to him.

"Now all of you hurry up and give me the begging money," says Anand Bhai. "I want to steal Mohan's car tonight. Hope it's in good condition so I can sell it fast. Jackpot—you want to buy a car?"

Everyone laughs. Soon, they all start to line up.

Handsome inches forward, the ball-bearing
wheels of his wooden platform unable to move
freely on the gravel. Anand Bhai looks at the old
man who sits near the goat. The old man has lit
yet another beedi, but he throws it away immediately and picks up what he was sitting on—a metal
box. He walks towards Anand Bhai and places the
metal box on the gravel.

Handsome states the amount he earned. Anand
Bhai gives Handsome his share. The rest goes into
the metal box. Handsome vigorously scratches his
head with both hands as though he has not washed
in weeks.

When it is Jackpot's turn, Anand Bhai tousles
the boy's hair. Jackpot is younger than Pushpa at
the orphanage, Chamdi thinks, and yet he knows
so much. Chamdi stares at Anand Bhai's bloodshot eyes and the sweat on his chest. Even though
they are out in the open, the smell of beedis is
very strong. Perhaps it is because there is no wind.
The air is old and it refuses to leave.

Handsome draws Anand Bhai's attention to
Chamdi.

"So who are you?" Anand Bhai asks Chamdi.

"He's new here," says Sumdi. "We brought him
to take your blessing."

"I'm asking the boy."

"My name is Chamdi."

"Chamdi? What sort of name is that?"

Chamdi knows his answers must be brief. A lack of respect will result in blood.

"My father gave me that name."

"Where's your father?"

"Dead."

Chamdi is surprised at the speed of his answer. But he will never reveal that he is looking for his father.

"Did Sumdi explain the rules to you?" questions Anand Bhai.

"Yes."

"Explain them back to me."

"Everything we make is yours."

"Lovely rule."

"Then you give us back whatever you feel is right."

"And you saw what happened to Munna—he didn't follow rules. He carried a knife. He disrespected me. Now for a while you will beg. Get to know your area really well. Then slowly you will progress to stealing. No stealing until you are trained."

"Yes."

"Yes what?"

"Yes, Anand Bhai."

"Good."

"Tonight was your first night and I'm in a good mood. So you keep whatever you earned."

Chamdi is glad to hear that. But he corrects himself immediately. He is not proud of the way he has earned his money.

Anand Bhai turns to Sumdi. "So—how are my eyes doing? Have they seen anything useful?"

"Yes," says Sumdi. "On Lamington Road there's a jeweller shop. Every Monday, in the afternoon at around three, this young woman comes to buy jewellery. She looks like she is newly married. Only the driver is with her and he's not very strong. I have seen for a month now, and she is there every week on Mondays, without fail."

"Hmm. We'll do some setting."

Sumdi tells Anand Bhai how much money he made. He gets his share and deposits the rest in the metal box.

Then Anand Bhai asks Guddi: "Did you sell anything today?"

"One Laxmi, one Hanuman, one Ganesha," she replies.

A wail erupts from the room to their left. A glow emanates from the open window—it is the light of a natural flame, an oil lantern perhaps.

Anand Bhai clicks his tongue. "Darzi must be sewing Munna up," he says to Guddi. "So you can't enter the room now. But the old woman has made more gods for you. Go to her tomorrow morning."

"Yes, Anand Bhai."

"Don't worry, Munna's a tough boy."

Anand Bhai says this to himself as if he now regrets slashing Munna. They all stand in silence and listen for more wails. As Chamdi stares at the room, he sees shadows on the wall, vague shapes, and he understands now why the man is called Darzi. He is Anand Bhai's tailor, the one who does the dirty stitching. Darzi must be taking a needle and thread and sewing Munna up while Chottu holds Munna. He wonders if Darzi is a real doctor—probably not. He hopes Munna gets some medicine for the pain.

"I'll go and see how Munna is," Anand Bhai says. "You all go home." He turns to Sumdi. "On the way feed Dabba. Here's some money, buy him mutton chops. I don't think anyone has gone to him since yesterday. And tell him I will come for information later tonight. He'd better have something."

As Anand Bhai is entering Darzi's room, a large white car pulls up in the square. The driver keeps the engine running and the car's headlights blaze onto the gravel, and Chamdi can see every stone and pebble. The back door of the car opens and out steps a boy. Chamdi is glad that the boy is not deformed in any way. In fact, the boy looks very clean, as though he has been scrubbed thoroughly. His blue T-shirt and white shorts seem brand new. He is as young as Chamdi, and his features are very soft, and his hair falls over his eyes. Chamdi says to himself that this boy could easily be mistaken for a girl.

Anand Bhai comes out of Darzi's room and goes to the driver's window. The windows are tinted. A male hand drops a packet into Anand Bhai's palm and the window closes. Anand Bhai digs the packet into the front of his black trousers and watches as the car turns and drives away.

The boy stands still for a moment. Then he walks quietly towards Anand Bhai. As he walks, the boy looks at Chamdi, probably because he has spotted somebody new. Chamdi smiles at the boy, but the boy does not return the smile. He simply walks lifelessly across the gravel as if he has nowhere to go. Then suddenly the boy collapses to the ground, and Chamdi rushes to his aid. As he bends down to help the boy, he notices the boy's white shorts. There is a dark patch of blood on them and drops of blood trickle down his thigh. Chamdi cannot take his eyes off the blood. He wonders why the boy is bleeding. Anand Bhai crouches down and taps the boy lightly on his cheeks. For a moment, Anand Bhai's eyes lock into Chamdi's. Anand Bhai smiles, and Chamdi looks away. Anand Bhai picks the boy up and carries him to his room.

Sumdi leads Chamdi away from the adda. This time, the three of them take a new route. Chamdi trails them, and pays little attention to his surroundings. He is trying hard to forget the boy. Even though he has seen so many deformed people, there was something about this boy that disturbed him. He does not understand why Anand Bhai smiled at him, and why that smile made his skin crawl.

"Who was that boy?" asks Chamdi after a while.

Guddi picks up a broken twig from the ground and chucks it onto the wall that surrounds a building compound. There is an advertisement for Lifebuoy Soap painted on the wall.

"Who was that boy?" Chamdi asks again. "There was blood on him . . ."

"That was Khilowna," answers Sumdi.

What strange names these people have, thinks Chamdi. Handsome and Jackpot's names do not match their appearance at all. And now this boy is called a toy.

"Why is he called Khilowna?" he asks.

"Look—do you have to know everything?" snaps Guddi.

"I just . . ."

"He must know," says Sumdi. "Let him know. The boy is called Khilowna because grown men play with him. They hurt him in dirty ways. The blood you saw, that was because . . ."

"Sumdi . . ." interrupts Guddi.

"Anyway, he belongs to Anand Bhai. He looks pretty, but he's filthy, he's . . ."

"That's enough," says Guddi.

There is a look of disgust on Sumdi's face. Chamdi thinks he understands what Sumdi has just told him. But not entirely. He feels sorry for the boy, and then very afraid. But he does not fully understand his fear.

They all remain quiet for a while. A watchman taps his large cane on the ground and patrols the building compound. He notices the three of them and starts tapping loudly. Sumdi slows down on purpose. It seems to bother the watchman, but he does nothing.

"I want to feed Moti," says Guddi.

"He's a dog. He can take care of himself," says Sumdi.

"But he's not well."

"Not now. Later."

Guddi does not argue. She walks with her head down. Chamdi is sorry that he asked about Khilowna. It seems to have made Sumdi angry. Chamdi wishes he had not seen Khilowna at all. Why did Anand Bhai smile at Chamdi like that? He distracts himself by eyeing a packet of cream biscuits that hangs from a blue rubber sling in a beedi shop. A few packets of sliced bread are stacked on the counter.

Just in front of the beediwala is a man who sells mutton chops. His face is dark and sweaty as a result of the coal of the iron grill. Chamdi stares at the beads of sweat on the man's face. The man exchanges greetings with Sumdi, who takes out the ten-rupee note that Anand Bhai gave him and hands it to the man.

"Are you okay?" Guddi asks Chamdi.

"No, I . . ."

"You'll be okay," she says. "Once you live on the streets, you see everything in a few days. You see in a few days what most grown-ups see in a lifetime. That's what my father used to say. Don't worry."

"Yes," replies Chamdi. "Thank you."

It is the first time she has spoken to him gently since the night she found him. The man twirls the mutton skewers and wipes his face with his shirtsleeves.

"Now you'll meet Dabba," she says. "I like Dabba."

"Who's Dabba?" asks Chamdi.

"Dabba's a beggar. He's been with Anand Bhai for very long."

"But why is Anand Bhai asking Sumdi to feed him?"

"You'll see."

Chamdi does not like that this man is called Dabba. It means he must resemble a box. This time Chamdi does not ask. It is best he leaves their names alone.

When they are ready, Sumdi takes the mutton chops that are wrapped in a newspaper. He puts one in his mouth and immediately spits it out on the paper. "Hot," he gasps. The man laughs, the crackling coal of the grill giving birth to new sweat on his face. As they walk away, Guddi flips a piece of mutton from hand to hand. She blows on it, and then, even though it is still steaming, she eats it. Sumdi gobbles down a piece as well. He holds out the meat to Chamdi.

"Eat while it's hot," he says.

"Isn't this Dabba's food?"

"Delivery charge. Now stop being a saint and eat."

"Don't feed Chamdi," says Guddi sternly. "He has to fit in through the temple bars."

"Let him eat," says Sumdi. "Otherwise the fool will faint while running."

Chamdi does not wait for Guddi's approval. He savours the taste of the mutton as it melts in his mouth. "First time in my life I'm eating mutton," he says.

"What?" asks Sumdi.

"At the orphanage all we had was vegetables, rice, and dal."

"It sounds like a horrible prison."

"No, it was good. We had beds. We learned how to read and write."

"You and your reading and writing. What a waste! Tell me, if Munna knew how to read and write, would he have been able to prevent the knife from gouging his eye out?"

"The eye was gouged? It came out?"

"I hope so."

Chamdi is shocked. "Why?"

"I don't like Munna. He wants to be a don someday. Talks of cutting and killing all the time."

"But Munna might go blind, no?"

"Who knows? Anyway, did you like the mutton?"

"I did."

"You know what mutton it was?"

"Meaning?"

"What mutton—cow, goat, lamb . . ."

"I don't know."

"It was dog meat."

"What?"

"These vendors kill stray dogs and cook their meat."

Chamdi stares at Sumdi in horror. Could this be another one of Sumdi's pranks? Chamdi turns to Guddi to gauge her reaction. But she is not laughing.

"Would I eat a dog?" she asks Chamdi. "You saw how I feel about my Moti. Would I eat Moti?"

"Thank God," says Chamdi. "I felt sick."

"I only eat dogs I don't know," she says.

Sumdi's gleeful laugh cuts through the night air. He wraps the rest of the mutton chops in the paper, then hits his sister on the back. She hits him back hard. How can they be so relaxed after what they have just witnessed? It is as if Chamdi cannot fully absorb this strange new world.

"I don't understand something," he tells Sumdi.

"Yes, say."

"If Anand Bhai can make money stealing cars, why does he need beggars?"

"Begging is a big business, that's why."

"So all the money, does it make him rich?"

"More important than that, it keeps *us* poor. We don't die of hunger, but we wish we did. Men like Anand Bhai make sure we have no way out. We are too afraid to get real work because he will come after us. We bring him money, we bring him information. Once you fall into this trap, it becomes your life. That's why we are stealing the temple money. We want to get out of this hell."

"What if he catches us?"

Sumdi does not answer. The three of them find themselves on a main road again. This road is full of sari shops and jewellery shops. There is a police station as well. It has blue and yellow stripes on its pillars. What a strange tiger that would make, Chamdi thinks.

A police-tiger.

Chamdi is excited by the thought. Perhaps the real, living policemen of Bombay need strong tigers to help them keep Bombay safe. One day, the walls of these police stations will shake and tigers will emerge from their pillars and patrol the streets. Then we will see who riots, thinks Chamdi.

He wants to tell Sumdi and Guddi this, but Guddi slips away, starts walking in another direction. Sumdi does not seem to mind. Chamdi feels Guddi's mind is on Moti. He likes that she cares about a sick stray dog even though she hardly has any food for herself.

Soon, Sumdi and Chamdi come to a halt just outside a jeweller's shop called Shree Satyam Jewellers. The shop is closed for the night and the streetlights cast tall shadows on its brown doors. Its steel shutters reflect light grudgingly, and Chamdi can see that an iron padlock binds the shutters together. Sumdi leads him into a narrow alley beside the shop. Electrical wires and the building's pipes are exposed, and water drains out of the thickest one. It falls onto a human head.

As Chamdi's eyes adjust to the dim light in the alley, he discerns a man with very little hair on his head, and absolutely none on his body. This man has no arms or legs. He is merely a square piece of human being. He lies flat on his back on the ground and he has no choice but to let the water, or whatever it is, fall on him. When he hears his visitors, he turns his head sideward and opens his eyes. A foul smell emanates from him.

"Dabba," says Sumdi. "Food."

The moment he hears the word "food," Dabba's mouth opens. His eyes closed tight, he waits. Sumdi puts a mutton ball in his mouth. Dabba chews on it quickly and swallows it. He opens his mouth again. Sumdi puts the second piece in. A scrap of cloth is wrapped around Dabba's waist. It is filthy, but it prevents him from being naked. He is simply a head and a breathing torso. Dabba has finished eating the third and final piece of mutton. He licks his lips and opens his eyes wide. A few drops of water fall onto his chest.

"Can you move me?" he asks Sumdi. "Since yesterday this pipe has been leaking and torturing me."

Sumdi nods at Chamdi. "Help me lift him," he says.

Dabba looks to be about fifty. His eyes are kind, thinks Chamdi. Perhaps that is because he is forced to stare at the sky all day. They have even acquired some of the blue-grey hue of an evening sky.

"Hold him and lift him up," commands Sumdi.

Sumdi holds onto one side of Dabba, the side where his head is. Chamdi holds Dabba from below the waist. They lift up the torso. Chamdi holds his breath—the smell is unbearable.

"We'll keep you here only," Sumdi tells Dabba.

They place him back on the ground, only a foot away from the leaking pipe. Chamdi checks his hands. They are clean.

"Who's the new boy?" asks Dabba.

"My friend Chamdi."

"Thank you for lifting me," says Dabba.

Chamdi nods. He cannot look into Dabba's eyes, even though they remind him of the sky.

"Sumdi," says Dabba. "Please scratch my chest. I'm going mad."

"Where?"

"Anywhere, please. I can't bear it anymore."

Chamdi looks at Dabba's dirty torso and wonders how Sumdi will get the guts to scratch him.

"There's a soda cap next to my face," says Dabba, as if he could read Chamdi's mind.

Sumdi picks up the jagged steel cap and scratches Dabba's chest.

"Aaah . . ." says Dabba. "Harder, harder."

"Tell me where."

"Everywhere! Tear my skin apart, I beg you."

Sumdi continues to trace the cap along every inch of Dabba's torso. In some areas, he uses more pressure than others. Chamdi realizes Sumdi has done this before because Sumdi can tell which of Dabba's groans are ones of pleasure and which are those of discomfort. Chamdi wonders how Dabba goes to the bathroom. But then the cloth is so filthy . . .

"Now the face," says Dabba, and closes his eyes in anticipation.

As Sumdi lifts his hand from Dabba's torso, Chamdi notices that the steel cap has left lines of blood.

"Anand Bhai sends a message," says Sumdi.

"My ears are open," says Dabba as he turns his face to the side he wants scratched.

"He will come tonight to meet you. He wants information."

"I have good news for him. Yes, good news. But I'm fed up. This time I'm going to bargain. I can't do this anymore. I want to live in peace."

"I understand," says Sumdi.

"Now even the ears please, do the ears."

"I must go," says Sumdi. "I have to feed Amma."

"Okay. Before you go, come here. I want to tell you something."

He whispers into Sumdi's ear, then lets out a heavy sigh.

"Promise me you will do as I have asked," says Dabba. "In case Anand Bhai does not agree, I need your help."

"I . . . I will try," says Sumdi.

"Thank you, Sumdi. I can sleep now, I can sleep."

Sumdi throws the steel cap away and pats Dabba on the chest. He leads Chamdi out of the lane.

Chamdi looks over his shoulder as Dabba twitches
like a worm on the ground.

"What did he tell you?" asks Chamdi.

"Leave it."

"He smelled very bad. How does he go to the
toilet?"

"Wherever he is, that's the toilet."

"So who washes him?"

"Anand Bhai does not want anyone to wash
him. The more he smells, the more people will
leave him alone. When Anand Bhai allows, we
take a bucket and throw water on him. Make him
fully wet, that's all."

"Poor man."

"He may be poor, but he makes a lot of money
for Anand Bhai."

"Through begging?"

"Anand Bhai's real money comes from rob-
beries. He put Dabba next to the jeweller's shop
so that he can hear conversations, any important information. As long as no customers can
see him, the jeweller does not pay attention
to Dabba because he's like a leper. Soon he
finds out exactly when the consignment comes,
what time, where the money is kept, everything.
Each time Anand Bhai wants to rob a place, he

will pick up Dabba in a jeep and keep him at that location."

"So Dabba works as Anand Bhai's ears, like you are his eyes?"

"Right."

"So why does he not look after you all well?"

"Because if one Dabba dies, he will make another."

"What do you mean?"

"You think he was born like this? Dabba was a normal man. He was a waiter in an Irani restaurant. One day a taxiwala rammed into him. Dabba lost both his legs. Till today he says the menu out loud to pass the time."

Chamdi is about to ask how Dabba lost his arms too, but realizes he has some idea of how that happened. He understands now why the man is named Dabba.

Anand Bhai makes boxes out of human beings.

EIGHT

Chamdi is unable to sleep. He keeps imagining
Dabba wiggling on the ground to satisfy an itch.

On the main road, the streetlights are harsh.
Their light falls on the bus stop, on a poster of a
politician dressed in white. A taxiwala has parked
his taxi halfway on the footpath and has gone to
sleep in the back seat. Only the soles of his feet
are visible, poking out of the rear window. A
group of poorly dressed children runs past the
taxi. A small boy leads the pack. He carries a
packet in his hand. He has quite a lead over the
rest of them. Then he stops and sits down on the
footpath. As he pants heavily, he opens the packet

to reveal biscuits. The rest of the girls and boys join him and start eating. He gets hit on the head by an older girl, but he does not hit back. Instead, he gives her a smile full of mischief.

Chamdi is about to cross the street and talk to these children when he hears a voice.

His body tightens and he stays very still just to make sure that he did indeed hear it—a voice as warm as the night itself.

A song is alive.

He follows that song. It pulls him past the burnt building. As he walks, he takes note of the hole in the cement wall that he entered only a few hours ago to get to Anand Bhai's adda. Through the hole he can see the gravel of the small school playground. It could be a ghost-child who is singing, one of the schoolchildren perhaps. She misses her friends so she sings songs at night that will linger till morning and leave only when the school bell rings. He slowly passes through the hole in the wall. But the song escapes him as soon as he enters the playground. Instead, there is Guddi, sitting on the ground, leaning against the wall.

"What are you doing here?" she asks.

"Oh, it's you," says Chamdi.

An abandoned rubber chappal lies on the ground. A red hair ribbon crawls on the gravel. The branch of a tree scrapes against the glass window of a classroom.

"Was that you singing?" he asks.

"No," says Guddi.

"But no one else is around."

"Why are you awake?"

"I couldn't sleep," says Chamdi. "You have a beautiful voice. I know that was you singing."

He sits down next to her, cross-legged just like her.

"Why are you sitting so close to me?" she asks.

"It's so dark, I . . . I can't see."

"Don't worry, I'm not going to eat you."

"If you want me to go, I'll go."

"Up to you."

"Then I'll stay. Will you sing for me?"

"No."

"Please."

"I don't sing for anyone."

"Then I'll eat so much that I become balloon-sized. Then you'll have to find some other thin boy to do your work."

"Are you threatening me?"

"Yes."

"I'll knife you, you bloody dog. I'll cut you up into small pieces and sell them as Chamdi-meat. Don't ever threaten me again."

"My God . . ."

Guddi puts her hand on the gravel. The red hair ribbon blows near her and brushes her knee, but she does not touch it. She picks up a twig and makes gashes in the gravel.

"Please sing for me," says Chamdi.

"If I sing for you, will you promise to get that money from the temple?"

"No, I can't."

"Look at me," she says.

Chamdi looks at Guddi. She is probably the same age as he, but she seems older. She has lived under more sun, more dust, she has heard more truck horns than he, and she is the only girl he knows who has seen her father crushed by a car.

"Look into my eyes," she says. "Make a promise that no matter what, you will get that money for us. Once you look into someone's eyes and make a promise, it cannot be broken. Now look at me."

Chamdi looks into her brown eyes. He feels a tingle in his stomach. For a few seconds their eyes meet, and even though Chamdi wants to lower his, he is unable to do so until the promise is made.

"I promise," he says. *I promise I will get that money for you. But I don't think I can steal.*

Guddi throws the twig away and wipes her hands on her brown dress.

And begins to sing.

What follows is something Chamdi has never imagined.

Guddi's voice suggests that her throat contains magical things, impossible things. It is as though colours are singing, and each colour is a note. Chamdi's skin breaks into ripples, and if he could fly he would go straight into the glass windows of the nearby classroom and come out unharmed. Such is the beauty of Guddi's voice.

The leaves in the trees move gently, as though the trees have felt her song, and dust rises in the air, and swirls about in a playful dance.

By the time Guddi finishes, Chamdi knows that this song is the beginning of something unearthly. So he will use unearthly words to tell her how lovely the song is. He leans towards her and whispers in her ear, "*Khile Soma Kafusal.*"

"What?" she says, slowly catching her breath.

"*Khile Soma Kafusal,*" he repeats softly.

"What does that mean?"

"It is spoken in the Language of Gardens. Someday I will tell you what it means."

"Where is that language spoken?"

"In Kahunsha."

"Kahunsha?"

"The city of no sadness. One day, all sadness will die, and Kahunsha will be born."

As Chamdi whispers his secret to Guddi, he forgets, for a second, that it is night. Everything around him is luminous—the leaves, the red hair ribbon, the gravel is waiting to burst.

Guddi flicks the hair off her face and her brown eyes widen. Her eyelashes seem to lengthen—they stretch out as if to reach Chamdi.

"Don't be an idiot," she says. "How can such a place exist?"

"Because of your song. Your song is so beautiful that it has the power to create a whole new city."

"Have you lost your mind?"

"Yes. And I will lose it again, and again, and again, until we are happy. You, me, Sumdi, Amma, the baby, even Dabba. Someday, we will all live together in Kahunsha."

NINE.

A group of boys sit on a handcart and smoke.
Sumdi is amongst them, seated next to the
smallest boy, whose head is shaved. Chamdi
watches the boys pass a cigarette from hand to
hand, and wait for it to come back to them. One
of the boys has a tin can and he drums on it. The
bald one who sits next to Sumdi starts drumming
too, but he does so on Sumdi's polio leg, and
then puts his ear to it, as though he expects it to
emit a sound. The boys have a good laugh. Then
Sumdi starts to speak and Chamdi realizes that
Sumdi is telling them a story. It is about how
his ribs will one day turn into tusks. Chamdi

chuckles because Sumdi is doing a terrible job of telling the story.

Under a streetlight, Guddi stands with her hands by her side and smiles at Chamdi. The streetlight plays the part of the sun as it reflects light off Guddi's head. There is a dim glow from the room above Muchhad's bakery, and Chamdi is glad that he can hear no sounds from the room. He hopes that Muchhad and his wife are fast asleep, and that Muchhad's wife travels far in her sleep, goes to places she dreamt of as a child.

"Come with me," says Guddi.

"Where?"

"For a ride."

"What ride?"

Guddi starts walking, and Chamdi likes how she waits for no one. He is no longer scared of her. He knows that anyone who can sing like she can must have the lightest heart in the world.

Guddi does not look at him. She continues to walk past the closed shops. Chamdi walks a little faster to catch up with her, but then decides to let her lead him. The traffic lights are blinking red—on and off like eyes without sleep, he thinks. As they reach an intersection, a taxi swerves dangerously close to the footpath. Men are asleep on the footpath in a row, and even though the taxi's headlights flash on their faces, they do not stir.

Soon they pass the closed doors of a liquor bar. A dark man stands outside the entrance with his hands folded, and his fierce manner suggests that he is guarding the door. Two men smoke outside the bar, and it is obvious from how they struggle to stand that they are drunk. Chamdi notices the flimsy tin roofs of the shops. Large stones are kept on top of them to prevent them from being blown away by the wind.

Now Chamdi spies three children asleep on the steps of a pharmacy. Guddi kicks one of the boys lightly. The boy wakes up with a jerk, but the moment he sees Guddi, he smiles, hurls a curse, and rests his head back on the hard stone. This must be what Sumdi meant when he said that Bombay itself was an orphanage, thinks Chamdi. There are children just like him strewn all over the city. Chamdi wishes the streetlights were colourful—pink, red, purple, orange. Why not? They bend like trees anyway.

Guddi stops in front of a taxi that has smashed into a tree on the sidewalk. She bends down and hides behind the car. Being careful to watch out for glass, Chamdi takes the same position.

"What are we doing?" he asks.

"Hiding."

"From what?"

"Horses."

"There are horses here?"

"Yes. You like brown or black ones?"

"I . . . I've never seen a horse before."

"Tonight we'll go for a horse ride."

Is she teasing him? It is entirely possible. Later, she and her brother will have a mighty laugh. *The fool believed me when I told him there are horses on the street,* she will say.

"We'll have to wait. But they'll come for sure," says Guddi.

"Horses will come galloping on their own?"

"Not by themselves, you idiot. Ghoda-gadi!"

"A horse carriage at this time of night?"

"Yes. They do the rounds of Marine Drive by the sea. Once they've made their money there, then late at night they rest. The stables are nearby so the old man comes this way. We'll have to walk back to our kholi from the stables, okay?"

"Yes."

"You'll have to jump on. If he catches us, he'll use the horsewhip on us. So be careful."

"Have you done this before with Sumdi?"

"No, Sumdi cannot run."

"Oh . . . yes . . ."

"Anytime now he'll come."

Chamdi is excited at the thought of jumping onto a horse carriage. At the orphanage, the bravest thing he did was sneak out of the orphanage in the middle of the night and walk about in the courtyard. But he did not have the guts to venture into the city. Now, not only is he in the middle of the city but he is also about to ride through the city on a horse carriage.

As the two of them wait, crouched behind the smashed taxi, Chamdi feels renewed. He is in the middle of a dark road, and there are only buildings and shops and liquor bars around him, but Guddi's song has given him strength.

"Your song . . . it was really beautiful," he tells her. "Where did you learn it?"

"I made it up," she replies.

"Your song will start a whole new city and . . ."

"No," she cuts in. "It won't."

"Why not?"

"I made that song up after my father died. The day he died, as he was crossing the road, I called out his name and he turned back to look at me and that was when the car hit him. He was waving at me. I made the song up because of his death. So how can something like that start a new city?"

Chamdi stares at the tire of the taxi. The hub-cap is smashed in. The dent on the door of the driver's side gives the impression that the body of the car is made from black cardboard.

Suddenly she grips his hand. "Listen," she whispers.

Chamdi can hear nothing. Instead, he looks at Guddi's hands, at the dirt that is stuck on them, at the way her fingernails are eaten, at the orange bangles she never takes off, and he follows her hand up to the elbow and sees a faint trace of blood, probably the result of an itch she satis-fied too well, and then he sees the sleeve of her brown dress, and then he looks at her face, and he tells himself that even if she sang for her father, Chamdi has no doubt that the song will do what he wants it to.

"The horses are coming," whispers Guddi.

She holds Chamdi's hand, and he finds he cannot look in the direction of the horses. Guddi can tell that he is staring at her, so she places her hands on his head and turns it the other way, and they both peer above the hood of the taxi and see a tall carriage coming their way—two black horses striding, an old man smoking a beedi at the helm, a folded whip in his hand, and the four large wheels of the carriage spinning like worlds, bringing the horses closer and closer. Chamdi and Guddi wait for the carriage to pass and then they both run behind it. There is a hutch in the back, small enough for them to fit in, and Guddi gets on and sits down. She faces him now and stretches her arms out for him, and Chamdi tells himself that he does not want to get on that carriage, no, he will spend his entire life running behind this girl because the moment he steps onto that carriage her arms will no longer be outstretched. No one has ever done this for him, stretched out their arms, although he has dreamt of this moment many times, but in his dreams it has been his mother and father coming to the orphanage as he runs into their arms. He has never pictured a girl his own age with brown hair and yellow teeth, but this is better, so much better. He does not realize that the carriage is moving farther and farther away from him, and he does not care. All he wants is to carry this image in his brain for the rest of his life.

But Guddi is alarmed. She makes wild gestures with her hands, and Chamdi breaks his
reverie and runs as though he is running away
forever towards a better place. And soon he is
on the carriage with Guddi and they face the
city, leave it backwards. The skyscrapers of the
city seem very far away but their lights shine
brightly. The thick, heavy branches of trees lean
towards the centre of the road from either side.
Chamdi loves the *clip-clop* of the horses as they
walk briskly through the wide street. If only this
carriage would go all the way to the orphanage,
what a ride that would be. He wishes the stables
never come.

He wonders what this street is called. There is
a movie theatre—Super Cinema, the name says.
Opposite Super Cinema is another theatre, The
Shalimar. He loves these names and thinks of the
theatres as brothers—Super and Shalimar.

He looks up at the night sky. It is bluish in
parts. Moonlight lands on different parts of
their bodies—their heads, thighs, noses, knees—
and soon every part of their bodies is screaming for more light. Guddi claps her hands,
and Chamdi smiles so wide that every tooth is
showing. He can see the moonlight fall on the

tin roofs of the closed shops, hit the road and wipe out the night's tiredness. He begs the light to seep into his body until he is completely dripping.

And Chamdi strains to catch a glimpse of the horses because they too will soon be drenched in light. Their black skin will shine, and the streets will be illuminated by their mighty glow, and he wonders if that glow will wake people from their sleep, if it will make them tear open their windows, to see him and her, two children, mouths open, swallowing light. He hopes this a sight that will inspire grown-ups to run onto the streets and get wet in the maddest manner. He watches Guddi as she flicks his hair off his face and giggles, and he does not know what that giggle means, but it is almost as wonderful as her song, and he suddenly says to her, "Your name is not Guddi. Tonight, I will call you Bulbul. I name you after a nightingale." The two of them laugh and sputter, and Chamdi feels that the old man who rides the horse carriage must know that they are in the hutch of his carriage but perhaps he does not care, and the horses must know too as they continue to stride onward. And Chamdi wonders if it is possible for only two people in the entire world to be alive, because that is how he feels right now, and that is what he wants to say to her.

The boys on the handcart have gone. Only Sumdi remains, and he is scratching an itch on his foot. Chamdi cannot tell exactly what time it is, but it must be very late because the street has never looked this deserted. It amazes him how it transforms so quickly in the morning as though the street is an animal that wakes from its slumber.

"Where were you?" demands Sumdi.

"We went for a ghoda-gadi ride," says Guddi.

"Chamdi, did you see how big the horse's middle leg is?"

"Don't tease him," says Guddi.

"Don't tease him?"

"Let him be."

"Did Chamdi do some magic on you?"

"Let him be, I said."

"Chamdi," says Sumdi. "What did you do to my sister? Did you take out one of your ribs and use it as a magic wand so that she has changed her feelings? Don't get too carried away. She's my sister. If you touch her in any bad way, I'll cut your third leg, understand?"

"Where's Amma?" asks Guddi.

"She's sleeping."

Chamdi remains silent. Perhaps it is the contrast with the ride soaked in moonlight, but he notices again how dismal this area of the city is. The shops are packed too close to each other, the walls of the buildings are damaged, the windows are cracked in so many apartments, and even when plants grow, they creep along the building walls like thieves. What type of house makes plants feel like criminals?

"Is the whole of Bombay like this only?" he asks at last. "Old buildings, small shops, stray dogs, and beggars?"

"No," says Sumdi. "There's a huge garbage dump nearby which you have not seen."

"There's much more than this," says Guddi. "My father always said there's no place like Bombay."

"He was right," says Sumdi. "No place like this whorehouse."

"Shut up," says Guddi. "There's Marine Drive, a whole road by the sea lined by coconut trees, and at night you can see the buildings along the shore all lit up."

"Are there any gardens?" asks Chamdi. "Where's the nearest garden?"

"Hanging Gardens," says Guddi. "You'll love the Hanging Gardens. All the trees are cut in the shapes of animals. Tigers, elephants . . . And it is on a hill so you can see the whole of Bombay."

"Yes, Bombay's hole is very nice," says Sumdi. "Everyone has free entry but once you enter you cannot leave."

"Sumdi!" shouts Guddi.

Sumdi keeps quiet. Guddi plays with the orange bangles on her wrists. Then she looks up at Chamdi.

"There's one more thing," she says. "My favourite place in Bombay."

"What is it?"

"Apollo Bunder. It's near the sea. The Gateway of India is there. My father used to take me there. We used to sit on the sea wall and eat chana, and sometimes we would feed the pigeons and he would tell me exactly what they were saying . . . that if you climbed up and sat on the dome of the Gateway, you could see all the way across the sea to the next country."

"Which country is that?"

"I don't know . . . he never told me."

Guddi gazes at the ground again. Chamdi assumes she is thinking about her father. He is

thrilled with the information he has just received.
He wants to go to Marine Drive. He would love
to sit by the sea and watch how the sun makes the
water sparkle. And a whole line of coconut trees
swaying in the wind—he could watch them for
hours. Even Apollo Bunder sounds interesting.
What country lies on the other side? He would
sit on the dome of the Gateway of India with
Guddi and look far out to the horizon. They
might spot children just like them on the other
side, and they would wave out to each other for
hours. And the Hanging Gardens . . . trees in
the shapes of animals. Imagine a bougainvillea
horse! Chamdi cannot wait to see this place. He
was right about the Bombay that he dreamt. It
does exist somewhere.

"Can we go there now?" he asks.

"Go where?"

"Hanging Gardens."

"No," says Sumdi. "Get some rest. Both of you."

Guddi lies down on the ground obediently. Her
feet accidentally touch Amma's head, but Amma
does not stir. The baby rests on a plastic sheet
that is covered by a dirty cloth. A rat crawls past.
Chamdi gets up to drive it away, but it disappears
into a hole in the footpath before he can reach it.

He fears for the baby. He wishes it had a clean place to stay. No wonder it is sick, living alongside rats.

Guddi places her tin box on the hole that the rat escaped into. Guddi gives Chamdi a quick glance and just before she closes her eyes she says to him, "Tomorrow is the day."

Chamdi wishes Mrs. Sadiq were next to him right now, so she could offer him good advice. He knows what she would say, that it is wrong to steal. Jesus would have been of no use right now. Jesus always stayed silent.

"Go to sleep," says Sumdi.

"No, I'll stay awake for a while."

"And do what?"

"Think."

"About what?"

"Anything. I'll dream."

"How can you dream while you're awake?"

"That's the best kind of dream."

"You have to be drunk for that to happen. Or on ganja. But you must not even know what ganja is."

"No."

"Ganja is what poor people use to distract themselves from their miserable lives. But even that costs money."

"That's why I dream. Dreams are free."

"Why are you so strange? Why can't you be normal and spit on the road or shit in your pants?"

"Tell me, what's the one thing you really want in your life?" asks Chamdi.

"I want to leave Bombay."

"That's not a dream."

"Why not?"

"Running away is not a dream. Anyway that is Bulbul's dream."

"Who the hell is Bulbul?"

Chamdi looks at Guddi. She smiles and then closes her eyes quickly as though a massive bout of sleep has suddenly come over her.

"*She* is Bulbul?" asks Sumdi. "That terror, you called her a nightingale? You really *are* a dreamer. Now go to sleep."

"Not before you answer my question."

"Why can't you let me be? Go and talk to the rat if you are lonely. Here, I'll lift the box and you can enter that hole and dream in the dark."

"What's the one thing you really want?"

"You won't let me sleep till I answer your question, will you?"

"No."

"Okay, I'll tell you."

"Truthfully."

"Yes, truthfully." Sumdi glances over at his sister. Her eyes stay closed. Amma stirs and then settles. A police jeep rushes past the bus stop. Chamdi quickly imagines three blue-and-yellow-striped tigers roaring behind the jeep, serving as its siren. The police-tigers go to places the jeep cannot. They pick out the scent of thieves much better than any policeman. And they will look after the children of Bombay, treat them as their own cubs.

"Okay," says Sumdi, holding his stiff leg. "I'll tell you."

"Good."

"But you can never repeat this to anyone. Not even back to me. And after we have had this stupid conversation, you'll let me sleep in peace. Even if God comes and starts cooking mutton biryani in the middle of the road you'll not wake me."

"I promise."

"You see this leg of mine? I've never been able to run. Even when I walk, I feel heavy. It's as though all my anger collects in this leg and it gets heavier and heavier. Even when my father died, I couldn't run to him. I got there last, after Amma and my sister. Sometimes I just wish that I wouldn't feel so heavy. So I really wish, you know, a waking dream just like yours in a way, that I will one day . . . No, it's stupid. I'm sleeping."

"Go on, Sumdi."

"What's the point? What I wish for is impossible."

"Why wish for what's possible?"

"Is that so?"

"Yes, it's like that."

"I want to fly," he whispers. "That's my dream. I, Sumdi, will one day fly all over Bombay, see every gulley, see all the shops, movie theatres, gambling dens, brothels, cock fights, cricket matches, and once I am done, I will fly over the sea like a champion bird, and never ever stop. I will keep on flying for the rest of my life."

"That's a wonderful dream," says Chamdi.

"But it can never come true, so what's the use?"

Chamdi does not say anything. He wants to tell Sumdi about Kahunsha. How police-tigers will patrol the streets to keep them safe, how there will be flowers everywhere, how all the water taps will gush forth pure rainwater, and how, most of all, no one will be deformed and people will not hurt each other.

"Now I have a question for you," says Sumdi.

"Yes?"

"Why do you wear that scarf around your neck all the time? Even when it's boiling hot you never take it off."

"It's not a scarf," says Chamdi. "It's . . ."

Chamdi is not sure if he should tell Sumdi the truth about the cloth. Not that he does not trust Sumdi, but Chamdi would like to keep the real meaning of the cloth a secret until it leads him to his father. But he does not want to lie to Sumdi either.

"This cloth was given to me by Mrs. Sadiq, the lady who looked after me at the orphanage. It reminds me of her," he says. "It will bring me good luck."

"You're a strange one to believe in luck in a city like Bombay," says Sumdi. "But we'll need all the luck we can get to leave this place. So keep it on. We are depending on you. Now get some rest." He turns his back to Chamdi and lies down.

A strong wind starts to blow. It gets stronger and stronger, and makes Chamdi uncomfortable. Perhaps the wind is telling him something. Yes, it is telling him not to be a ten-year-old fool and believe in police-tigers or bougainvillea horses.

The Hanging Gardens are created by chopping plants down. The plants must scream in agony each time an animal is made.

He stands up and looks around him. The two coconut trees behind the bus stop sway back and forth because of the heavy wind. Their branches point to the sky in the same way an overturned umbrella does. What a strange night this has been. The horse carriage ride was beautiful. Even the moon was brighter than usual. And now, the sky is angry.

TEN

In the morning, the sky has the gloom of dusk. The doors of the bakery are open, and from where he lies on the street Chamdi can see a woman in the room above the bakery. She wears a pink scarf on her head, holds a small book in her hand, and she is mumbling to herself. Perhaps she is praying, asking for protection from her own husband.

Chamdi's back hurts. He is still not used to the uneven stone of the footpath. And it hurts for another reason, too—something has been creeping up his back all night, a thought, and it has finally settled down in his brain: *Today is the day I become a thief.* But he still hopes for a way out. There has to be.

After a while, Sumdi stirs and stands up.

"Going to get food?" asks Chamdi.

"No," says Sumdi. "I have to get something else first."

"What?"

"Rat poison."

"What for?"

Sumdi does not answer him, and Chamdi is left to wonder. He knows that rat poison will be of no use at all. It might kill one rat, ten rats at the most, but in a city of countless rats, what good will that do? Still, he does not question Sumdi's actions. After all, it is Sumdi's money. Chamdi has his own money, but it makes him uneasy to use any of it.

For a moment, Chamdi watches the taxis as they roll slowly past. Then he turns his attention to the apartment buildings that look out over the street. Most of the windows in the buildings are closed, perhaps because of last night's heavy wind. Only a few men stand at their windows and peer onto the street. Some wear white vests and scratch their underarms, and some of them have red lips from chewing paan. Even though paan is colourful,

Chamdi does not like the way it stains the lips and eventually the streets.

"Can I come with you?" asks Chamdi, finally.

"No," says Sumdi.

"Why not?"

"I have work to do."

"But I need to talk to you about this afternoon."

Sumdi walks away from the tree. Only when he is a fair distance away from the bakery does he cross the road. Chamdi follows in Sumdi's footsteps.

"The oil you'll need this afternoon is with us," explains Sumdi as he blows his nose. "I'll give you the bottle when we get back."

"Where did you get the oil?" asks Chamdi.

"I stole it from the beediwala near the temple."

Chamdi remembers the beediwala shutting the lid of the biscuit jar hard on his wrist on his first day in the city. In a way, Chamdi deserved it. After all, it is Chamdi who is going to use the stolen oil.

"The plan is simple," says Sumdi. "Guddi will sit outside the temple and sell the gods. I will be with her. You stay out of sight, behind the beediwala's shop. But make sure you can see us, okay? When Namdeo Girhe makes his entry, that's your signal to smear yourself with oil. As soon as his puja is done, he will leave with the priest. The temple will then be closed for a while. You slip in from a side window. This side window can't be seen from the street. Its bars are very close to each other, but you will be able to go through them. You'll also need a hammer. I'll place it on the ground just below the side window."

"What is it for?"

"The money is kept in a large plastic box. First throw the hammer in through the window, then enter, then smash the box."

"Where do I meet you after I get the money?" asks Chamdi.

"Grant Road Station," says Sumdi. "Walk through the school playground. Turn right, cross the street, and you will come to Grant Road Station. Go to Platform 1 and stand near the ticket window. We will bring Amma and the baby there. And wait there only. Even if we take time, you have to wait."

"I'll wait," promises Chamdi.

"And idiot," says Sumdi. "Make sure you put the money in your pocket in the temple itself. Only take the notes. No coins. And once you come out, walk easy like you are in a garden. Only if you are seen, then run. Only you know you are a thief, remember that. If your heart is beating fast, no one else will be able to hear it, so just relax. Before you come out of the window, peek through the bars. We'll be outside. So we'll give you a sign."

"What if the temple window is closed?" asks Chamdi.

"On the day of the puja, because of the extra incense, they keep the side window open. They have to let the fragrance out. And the thief in."

"I'm not a thief," says Chamdi sharply.

"Okay, okay."

"And why has no one robbed the temple in all these years?"

"No one has the guts to rob that temple."

"Why not?"

"First of all, everyone thinks it's a miraculous temple. So to rob it would be bad luck."

"What's the other reason?"

"The temple is under Anand Bhai's protection."

"Oh . . ."

"Namdeo Girhe uses Anand Bhai to beat people up during voting. Anand Bhai's gang is very powerful. During voting, this temple is used for paying bribes to the police. The policewalas come in to pray and go out rich."

"During the puja, Anand Bhai will be there?"

"He might. But don't worry. He'll be in a daze because he always drinks bhang."

"What's that?"

"A drug he puts in a glass of milk and swallows."

"If he finds out, we're dead."

"By the time he finds out, we'll be on a train. Any more questions?"

What if I am caught and beaten, what if my ribs cause me to get stuck between the bars, what if while I am entering the window the bars move on their own, come in closer, and crush me, what if I cannot find Platform 1?

"No, I don't have any questions," says Chamdi.

They enter the lane just behind a shop that sells car and truck tires. Next to it is Pushpak Books, and a group of schoolchildren line up outside it with their parents. Sumdi enters a small building. Its archway entrance is painted bright yellow, but the rest of the building is rundown and peeling. The iron grilles on the windows make the building look even more rusted. Sumdi and Chamdi are now inside a very narrow passageway.

Chamdi inhales deeply, takes in the smell of different foods. There is also the pungent odour of waste emanating from a square landing in the centre of the building that is open to the sky. The inhabitants of the building must throw their garbage here—Chamdi spots green plastic bags in that landing, along with lots of eggshells and banana peels.

Sumdi knocks on a door that has a sticker of Shiva on it. He gestures to Chamdi to stay out of view. The cobras that spurt from Shiva's locks remind Chamdi of Guddi's wooden box, and of how he longs to do honest work like Guddi.

The door opens. Chamdi cannot see who it is, but from the way the person coughs, Chamdi can tell it is a man.

"I've come for some medicine," says Sumdi.

"Hah?"

"Anand Bhai has sent me."

"Oh? I've not seen you before. What's your name?"

"Raju. I came here two weeks ago with Munna."

"So where's Munna?"

"He's not well. He got cut above the eye."

"But how come I still don't recognize you? With a face like yours . . ."

"Sahib, you were . . . drunk last time I came, that's why maybe."

"You two-foot swine. You must be right. Because I'm drunk right now! So, what do you want?"

"The rat medicine . . ."

The man slams the door in Sumdi's face. Chamdi has no idea why Sumdi is doing all this. The door opens again. The man gives Sumdi a small packet.

"Now give my respects to Anand Bhai. What did you say your name was?"

"Raju," says Sumdi.

"Raju," says the man, "may you kill many rats!"

The man shuts the door abruptly. There is the sound of him banging into furniture. Sumdi scurries down the passageway. As they pass the landing, Chamdi notices a tomato fall from one of the apartments above.

"Why did you lie to him about your name?" asks Chamdi.

"Because Anand Bhai did not send me."

"But that man will recognize you, no?"

"Munna normally comes to collect poison from here for Anand Bhai when he has to do his dirty work. Munna used to make fun of this drunkard.

He would joke about how the drunkard would be completely out, early in the morning. That's how I know. I've never come here before. I just tried my luck—I knew he would not charge money if Anand Bhai ordered it. Anyway, let's hope in his nasha the drunkard forgets that I came here at all."

Chamdi thinks of Raman at the orphanage, and how he would mumble to himself when he was drunk. But Raman would never bang into furniture. His only problem was that he would pass out.

Back on the street now, Chamdi steps on a wrapper for Liril soap. He holds the wrapper to his nose and takes in the scent. The soap at the orphanage hardly had a scent. It did its job and left instantly.

Soon, Chamdi's surroundings seem familiar: a post office, a jeweller's shop, a police station with blue and yellow stripes on its walls. Chamdi wants to run his hands across the striped pillars and walls. They are, after all, the skin of the police-tigers. How their muscles will ripple like waves, he tells himself. They will be the most ferocious beings anyone has ever seen and their roar will be heard all across the city.

Soon, he and Sumdi are back at Dabba's spot in the passage between the shop and the building with the broken pipes. A metal bowl of coins rests near his head. He looks at Sumdi and smiles. Sumdi does not smile back.

"Did Anand Bhai come?" asks Sumdi.

"Yes."

"So what happened?"

"I told him that I had the best information for him. I told him about the jeweller's shop being sold, and I was about to tell him the exact time and date they would be moving the jewellery from his shop to another location, but I didn't. I told him to let me retire, that if he just gave me enough money to eat every day, I would be satisfied. It's a small price for all the information I have given him. I said I just wanted to live in peace. I even told him that I could live with you, that you would look after me. I just want to stay in one place and not be moved around like an animal."

"Did he agree?"

"He laughed. He said, 'I made you and I will tell you when to retire.' Just as I thought. That madarchod will die a hundred deaths before he leaves earth, you mark my words, or my name is not Dabba."

"I'm sorry."

"Did you bring what I asked?"

"Dabba, I . . ."

"Don't fail me, Sumdi. I expected Anand Bhai to fail me, but not you. Did you bring it or not?" The manner in which Dabba twitches suggests that he is hungry for what Sumdi has.

"Yes."

"Where is it?"

Sumdi turns to Chamdi and makes a gesture with his head, a signal for Chamdi to leave. Chamdi moves away a bit, but does not take his eyes off Dabba.

"Show me the poison," says Dabba. Sumdi opens the packet of rat poison and empties the black pills onto his palm.

"Okay," says Dabba. "No formalities. Put it in my mouth."

"I can't," says Sumdi. "I can't do it."

Dabba tries to sit up, sit back—anthing. He tries to reach Sumdi's palm with his mouth, but his limbless body allows him hardly any movement.

"Sumdi, you are a cripple too. You are also a dog on the road like me and you have a long life to live, be sure of that. Someday you will need help.

So don't deny me. Just put it in my mouth and go," says Dabba. "Get out of here."

"I can't put it in your mouth," replies Sumdi. "Please . . ."

"Turn me around. Flip me over so that I rest on my stomach."

"But the ground will hurt your face."

"Just do as I say," snaps Dabba.

Sumdi rolls Dabba over until he is flat on his stomach. Dabba's face rests on one side.

"Now put the poison on the ground and get out," says Dabba.

Sumdi overturns his palm and limps out of the alley. Chamdi stares in horror as Dabba licks the ground.

In the mid-afternoon, Chamdi waits behind the beedi shop. He forces himself to read the advertisement for Happy Tailors that has been pasted onto the back of the beedi shop. A sketch of a man's shirt occupies most of the ad and the man has a huge smile on his face. There is a rose in the front pocket of the shirt, and at the bottom, a promise from the tailor himself: HAPPY TAILORS MAKE YOU HAPPY. A large nail sticks out of the poster and Chamdi is careful not to let it scrape him.

He has a perfect view of the temple from this position. The place looks nothing like a temple, thinks Chamdi. It is nothing more than a ground-floor apartment that has been converted into a temple. Only the yellow wall makes it stand apart from the rest of the building. Who knows for sure if Ganesha thinks of this apartment as home? What if he is forced to live here but does not want to? What if he is waiting for someone like Chamdi to rescue him? Then Chamdi would not be doing anything wrong. These are his thoughts as he watches the old woman make garlands outside the temple. Chamdi cannot hear her, but he can tell from the manner in which her head bobs that she is humming a song. She inspects the garland that she has just finished, holding it out as though it is a measuring tape. The sun is shining now and it gives the marigolds in the garland extra colour. The woman hangs the garland from the nail on the roof of her small shop, then rubs her eyes and opens them wide before starting a fresh garland. Chamdi wonders why she wears a plain white sari. A flower woman should be as colourful as her flowers.

He grips the bottle of stolen oil in his hand. What if the beediwala sees him? What if the man comes behind his shop to relieve himself? No, he would not leave his shop counter unattended.

From where he waits, Chamdi can keep an eye on Sumdi and Guddi, who stand outside the temple right next to the old woman's stall. Sumdi is shirtless and Guddi has a couple of gods in her hands, but her wooden box is not visible. Perhaps she did not bring her box because if they need to run, it will be difficult to carry the box.

Chamdi is glad that he has never been inside the temple. If he had stood face to face with Ganesha, stealing would be even more shameful than it is now. Chamdi knows Ganesha through an illustration he saw in *Chandamama*, accompanying a story about Ganesha's birth. One of the children had asked if Ganesha was real, and Mrs. Sadiq said that he was probably an invention, but Chamdi said no one could prove that. He went on to explain that Ganesha must be a kind, understanding god, his elephant ears large enough to listen to the problems of people from the farthest corners of India, his extra limbs able to comfort more than two people at a time. Today, Chamdi begs Ganesha to be forgiving. *Please place your trunk*

*on my head and bless me. Forgive me for being a thief. I promise
I will never do it again.*

A white Ambassador car with a red siren on
top stops just outside the temple's lane. A police
jeep accompanies the Ambassador. The door
of the Ambassador opens and a man dressed in
a white kurta steps out. Chamdi assumes that
this man is the politician. He can tell from the
manner in which the people around the man
fawn over him. Chamdi cannot remember the
politician's name, but it does not matter. He is
suddenly very scared. He had no idea the police
would be here.

Then Chamdi remembers what Sumdi told
him. If by chance Chamdi gets caught, he must
start crying immediately. He must bring whoever
has caught him to where Amma is and he must
say that Amma is his mother and all he wanted
to do was buy some food and medicine for her
and the baby. He must not worry. But Chamdi is
still afraid. It is true that a normal citizen might
slap him and let him go, but this is the police. He
hopes they leave soon. As soon as he thinks this,
a police inspector steps out of the jeep. He takes
off his cap and places it on the dashboard, then
follows the politician towards the temple.

The appearance of the politician was meant to be the sign for Chamdi to start smearing himself with oil. He now opens the cap of the oil bottle and pours some onto his shaking palm. He wishes he had not seen the police jeep. He wonders if Sumdi knew that a police jeep always followed the politician's car. Perhaps Sumdi chose not to tell Chamdi.

Chamdi's hands are sticky with oil, but he has forgotten to take off his vest. He removes it anyway and places it on the ground. For a moment he wonders if he should remove the white cloth from around his neck as well, but he decides against it. He made a promise to himself that he would untie the cloth only when he found his father.

He starts with his chest. He spreads the oil evenly, keeping an eye on the windows opposite him, even though he feels no one would care that he is putting oil over his body. He finds it hard to oil his back, but he manages. He is relieved that he has hardly eaten in the past two days—he has become even thinner. The fear rushes back: can he really go through with this? One hard strike of the policeman's stick on his chest and his ribs will be broken forever.

Chamdi glances up. The police inspector has suddenly disappeared from sight. Chamdi whips around. What if the policeman has smelt him and has crept up behind Chamdi to take him away? He is clearly not cut out for this—he would be willing to trade his fast legs for Sumdi's defective one.

The politician has now entered the temple. The policeman reappears in Chamdi's line of sight. He stands outside the temple, only a few feet away from Sumdi. Chamdi feels a flood of relief. Surely, Sumdi will now give up the plan altogether. He will see the policeman, realize it is stupid to attempt such a robbery, and walk away from the temple. They will find another way to make money. It might take them a while, but they have brains. They will figure out a way to save the baby and eventually leave the city.

At least ten men have entered the temple with the politician. Sumdi and Guddi continue to stand outside the temple window. They do not appear concerned about the policeman. Chamdi steps out from behind the beedi shop and walks towards Sumdi and Guddi. Yes, his back and chest are smeared in oil, but it does not matter now. He sees Sumdi spot him as he walks, marks the confusion on Sumdi's face. Guddi takes a few

steps in his direction, while Sumdi stays rooted
to the spot with his hands on his hips. Chamdi
knows she will call him a coward. He looks down
in shame, but then decides to look her straight in
the eye. He summons his courage and raises his
head—Guddi walks fast towards him.

In that split second, a great force throws
Chamdi face down on the ground. Large blocks
of cement fall from the sky. He covers his head
and stays down. After a few seconds, he lifts his
head into a curtain of thick, black smoke. White
dust has stuck to his body because of the oil. He
looks for Guddi. Chamdi realizes that he is now
standing. The temple window is a gaping hole
without bars. It is difficult for him to hear, and
when he sees a bundle on the ground he screams,
but he cannot hear his own cry. It is Sumdi,
face down, his back torn open. Chamdi staggers
towards Sumdi, but his feet have no strength. He
slumps to the ground. He still cannot hear anything. He crawls forward, reaches out and turns
Sumdi's head sideways. Sumdi's mouth is bleeding. Chamdi drops the head. Now his hearing
comes back to him in bits. He hears a few muffled
moans, and says softly, "Guddi, Guddi." He gets
up from his knees and looks around. Stepping

towards the sound of the moans, he trips over the body of a man and scrambles away in fear, only to be blocked by a slab of cement. A brass temple bell lies on its side, shoes and slippers are strewn across the street, and he still cannot find Guddi. There is an arm lying on the street, with a watch on the wrist. Then he sees a figure in a brown dress, crawling away from him, towards what used to be the temple. He moves towards her and holds her by the waist. She is scared by his sudden touch and she screams. He says, "It's me, it's me," but when she looks at him, he realizes that this is not Guddi, but a grown woman. He lets go, and the woman crawls away. A man beside him writhes in pain. Large shards of glass are stuck in the man's neck and stomach. Chamdi coughs and covers his mouth to prevent dust from entering his lungs. He is about to keel over when he sees the wheel of a cycle. A hand rests on the wheel. There are orange bangles around the wrist. He is propelled towards the owner of this hand, even though his legs want to collapse. He gently lifts her head.

Blood flows from her nose, and there is a deep gash on her forehead. He looks around for help, but he is surrounded only by cries. He shakes her and utters her name, but she does not respond.

The blood from her nose is now on her lips. He must take her to the doctor's dispensary. He tries to lift her but she is heavy, so he drags her by her arms. Maybe he should not be pulling her by the arms. What if they are broken? He bends down, summons all the strength he has, and hoists Guddi on his shoulders. He searches for the door to the dispensary. Three men run towards him, but they pass him by as though he does not exist. They run towards the white Ambassador, which is in flames. The police jeep is overturned.

Chamdi reaches the door of the dispensary, but it is closed. He carefully places Guddi on the steps of the dispensary and pounds on the door. He wants to shout for help, but is unable to. Instead, his pounding becomes louder and louder. Why is the doctor not opening the door? He kicks the door hard and finally his voice comes to him, and he screams, but it is not exactly a word, it is a howl, and his fists join the howl, raw and hurt from beating on the door. He looks around him and suddenly knows: no one can help him. He sits. For a while, he sits on the steps of the dispensary as though nothing is wrong at all. He simply stares at the wound in the temple. Two stray dogs stand near him. It is difficult to breathe. He does

not look at Guddi. It is easier for him to look at
the dogs instead and the dogs are quiet.

Finally, Chamdi moves. He wipes the blood
off Guddi's face with his hands. The air around
him is still a chaotic mass of smoke and dust, and
through the haze, Chamdi thinks he sees Sumdi,
face buried in the ground. He quickly forces
himself to look away. He sees another body—the
old woman who makes garlands. She lies on the
ground covered in marigolds and lilies, and her
white sari is red with blood.

Guddi is not dead, he tells himself. She cannot
be. He knew no good could come from robbing
a temple. He looks at the gash in her forehead—it
is similar to Munna's gash. With this thought,
he stands up. There is only one person who can
help Guddi.

If Darzi fixed Munna, he can fix Guddi.

The adda is not far, he tells himself. I can reach
it. He jumps down the steps of the doctor's dispensary and runs, runs faster than when he fled
the orphanage. This is as fast as he would have
run had he robbed the temple, but now something
more precious than money is at stake. But even
though he runs faster than he ever has before, his
vision begins to fade. The shops around him spin

and his knees buckle, and soon he is flat on the ground. The last thing he sees is the sky—a black sky in the middle of the afternoon.

As Chamdi regains consciousness, he is gripped by fear. But it takes him only a second to remember why he is afraid. An old man reaches out and touches him. Chamdi takes the old man's hand and stands up. Satisfied that none of the shops are spinning, he starts walking fast. Soon the walk turns into a run, and once again his silver body is streaming through the street. He wonders if he is running in the right direction and is relieved when he sees Pushpam Collections—the air-conditioned clothing store—and the New Café Shirin Restaurant. In the distance, he can spot the tree he sleeps under. People pass him by, moving swiftly away from the temple. A man who runs a pharmacy slams the shutter down. When Chamdi hears the siren of an ambulance, worry grips him.

Chamdi finds it very hard to breathe, and he is surprised because he has run only a short distance. But he soon tastes the dirt in his mouth and realizes that his nostrils are blocked by grit. There is nothing he can do about it. He cannot

afford to stop. He tells himself that he does not
need air to run. He needs fast feet.

He cuts across the lane in front of his tree
and runs past the burnt building. He sprints
through the hole in the wall, enters the playground. He is surprised to find boys in white
shirts and khaki shorts, and girls with blue
ribbons in their hair. They are running too,
a game of sakli, hands held together to form a
chain, trying to catch a boy who is just out of
reach. It is as though they are not aware of the
blast. Their game temporarily stops as Chamdi
tears through them.

He soon comes to Anand Bhai's adda. He
rushes towards Darzi's room and bangs on the
closed door. There is no answer. He continues
to bang. The door opens suddenly. It is Anand
Bhai. Chamdi does not know what to say. He did
not expect Anand Bhai to open the door. He is
shirtless and hairy.

"Madarchod, who is it?" he asks, as he stares
down at Chamdi.

"It's me, Chamdi . . ."

Chamdi realizes he must be unrecognizable—
he has white dust all over him. His eyelashes stick
together and he blinks rapidly. He sticks one

finger in his eye and rubs hard. "I'm Sumdi's friend," he explains.

"What do you want?"

"There was a blast in the temple," says Chamdi.

"I know. Now get out."

Chamdi can hear moans of pain from inside the room, but he focuses on Anand Bhai.

"Guddi is hurt," says Chamdi. "Please save her."

"Everyone's hurt," says Anand Bhai. "Now get out."

"Please ask Darzi . . ."

Anand Bhai slams the door shut. Chamdi cannot believe it. His chest heaves up and down and he notices there is some blood on it. It must be Guddi's blood. Perhaps he should not have left Guddi alone. What if someone mistakes her for dead and takes her body away? If only Sumdi were with him, Sumdi would find a way to save Guddi. He must get Darzi's attention. Perhaps he is a kind man and will have pity on Chamdi. He bangs on the door again with great might. He is worried that Anand Bhai might slash him with a knife as he did Munna. But Guddi's life is worth any risk. This time Chamdi knows he has to somehow get Anand Bhai's attention so the door is open long enough for Darzi to notice Chamdi. But what should he say?

Anand Bhai opens the door again.

"I told you to leave!"

"I have information for you," says Chamdi.

"What information?"

Before Chamdi has time to think, a name jumps out of his mouth: "Dabba."

"What about Dabba?"

"Dabba is dead. He ate rat poison."

"He killed himself?"

"I saw it with my own eyes."

"So?"

"Dabba told me a secret."

For a moment, Anand Bhai stands still. He holds on to the door of the room and looks hard at Chamdi.

"Dabba told me a secret about the jeweller." Chamdi tries to remember the name of the jeweller's shop, but his memory fails him. "The jeweller who is selling the shop. I know on what day and exactly at what time he will be moving the jewellery."

"Listen to me, Chamdi. If you are lying, I will strangle you right here, right now."

Anand Bhai's mouth is very close to Chamdi's.

There are two grains of white rice stuck in Anand Bhai's beard as though he was eating in a hurry, or had to abandon his meal.

"Please," begs Chamdi. "Ask Darzi to save Guddi. I will tell you everything."

"First tell me what Dabba said."

"Dabba said that the jeweller will move the jewels tomorrow."

"What time?"

"That I will tell you only after you save Guddi."

Anand Bhai slaps Chamdi hard across the face. His hand lands on Chamdi's ear and there is a ringing sound that rises and seems to enter Chamdi's brain.

"No one bargains with me, understand?" snaps Anand Bhai.

"What's wrong with Guddi?" says a woman's voice.

The voice comes from inside Darzi's room. An old woman grips the open door for support. There are folds on her face, as though it is made of leather, and her eyes are narrow slits.

"Go inside," Anand Bhai tells her.

"What's wrong with Guddi?" she asks again.

"She's hurt very badly," says Chamdi. "She'll die if you don't help her. There was a blast . . ."

"We know," she says. "Anand, go get Guddi."

"Do you want me to save the bloody world?" yells Anand Bhai. "Your own son is bleeding in that room. Why don't you look after him?"

"Navin will be fine. He's being looked after. You get Guddi."

"What do you care about Guddi?"

"Anand. Get her. *Now.*"

Anand Bhai goes inside Darzi's room and comes back with a white shirt in his hand.

"Do you have a mother?" Anand Bhai asks Chamdi.

"No," says Chamdi.

"Good," says Anand Bhai. He looks at the old woman as he says this. Then he turns his attention to Chamdi. "I'll deal with you later. Let's get Guddi."

"But Darzi . . ."

"Darzi is looking after my brother. Now do you want to save Guddi or not?"

"We'll have to run fast," says Chamdi.

"No running."

Anand Bhai takes out car keys from the pocket of his black trousers. He puts on the white shirt but does not bother closing the buttons. They walk to the white car parked behind Darzi's room. Anand Bhai does not hurry. Chamdi swallows his anger and looks at the ground, noticing how tomatoes and cucumbers have been planted in the small space directly under Darzi's window. He forces himself to breathe. Then he reaches out and tries to open the door of the car, but it is locked.

"Hurry up!" explodes Chamdi. "She'll die."

"If she is meant to die, she will. But let me explain something to you. If you are lying about Dabba . . ."

"I'm not lying," says Chamdi. "I swear." For once in his life, he does not feel bad about lying, even though he gets a sick feeling in the pit of his stomach when he thinks about what Anand Bhai will do when he finds out.

Anand Bhai starts the car and opens the passenger door. Chamdi gets in, and before he can close the door, they speed off. They race along the road behind the adda, past a vegetable seller who carts his vegetables on wheels. Anand Bhai takes the bend, turns left. His right hand is on the steering wheel and his left hand is on the horn. He keeps the horn pressed, giving it the urgency of a siren. But there is no need. The street is deserted. The bomb has scared everyone into their homes. Chamdi is relieved. "Keep breathing, Guddi, keep breathing," he mutters. He does not care if Anand Bhai can hear him.

Anand Bhai wipes his hands on his trousers, then glances over at Chamdi, noticing the oil on Chamdi's body. Soon Anand Bhai's eyes are back on the road again. They pass the New Café Shirin Restaurant. Chamdi is surprised to see that the glass in most of the apartment building windows is shattered. An ambulance is parked near the temple, plus three police jeeps. Anand Bhai stops the car.

"Get out," he says. "The car can't go any further."

Chamdi and Anand Bhai run past the ambulance. Two men carry a body on a stretcher—that of a middle-aged man dressed in a white shirt and trousers. The skin on his face melts like wax and his eyes are closed. The two men dump him into the ambulance and rush back for more bodies.

They are near the temple now and Chamdi can see the old woman who sold garlands. She is still on the ground. Blood is splattered on the walls of the building opposite the temple. There is glass all around and loud moans of pain from every direction.

Guddi lies where Chamdi left her, motionless on the steps of the dispensary. Anand Bhai puts his finger against her mouth.

"She's alive," he says.

For the first time Chamdi appreciates the words that come out of Anand Bhai's mouth. He almost forgets his fear.

Anand Bhai hoists Guddi on his shoulders and walks towards the car.

"Sumdi is also here," Chamdi says.

"Hah? Sumdi also? Bhenchode . . . is he hurt?"

He goes towards the spot where Sumdi lies. He passes a small boy, a few years younger than Chamdi, trapped under a cement slab. Three men, including one policeman, are trying to lift the slab. The boy has passed out.

Now Chamdi can see Sumdi's torn-open back.

"He's gone," says Anand Bhai behind him.

"I won't leave him here," says Chamdi.

"No use. He's finished."

"We must take him also."

"I'm not wasting time on dead bodies."

Anand Bhai runs towards the ambulance with Guddi slung over his shoulder. Chamdi looks down at Sumdi. It is as though Sumdi is playing a prank. He has painted himself red and has somehow torn open his back. Chamdi looks around to see if anyone can help him carry his friend, but there is no one. He does not want to ask the men with the ambulance. The ambulance people do not save lives, he thinks. They only collect the dead.

He yanks Sumdi by the arms and drags him. Sumdi's neck is limp and his face almost touches the ground. Chamdi cannot bear to look at his friend's face. Teeth fall out of Sumdi's mouth.

"I told you to leave him," says Anand Bhai.

Chamdi continues to pull his friend's body until he loses his grip and Sumdi's body lands with a thud. Chamdi lifts Sumdi by his wrists once again.

The next minute Anand Bhai lifts Sumdi and hoists him over his shoulder. The ambulance men stare for a second and then move about their business. A policeman looks at Anand Bhai as well, but does nothing. He thumps the ambulance on the back twice and sends it on its way.

The back door of the car is open. Guddi lies in the back seat. Anand Bhai throws Sumdi to the floor of the car, and Chamdi wonders if the fall will break any of Sumdi's bones. He cannot bring himself to admit that it does not matter anymore.

He sneezes hard as the dust tickles his nostrils. The street is still empty of traffic, as if it is early in the morning. Most of the shops have closed, and few people walk on the street or look out from apartment windows.

Chamdi wonders why he does not feel like crying. He still feels this might be a game—all that red paint, and Sumdi and Guddi still as statues, pretending they are dead.

ELEVEN

Chamdi strains his eyes to adjust to the darkness. Grey cement walls make the room feel smaller than it is. There is a bathroom in one corner with a wooden door, slightly ajar, and Chamdi sees a red bucket on the bathroom floor. On one side of the room is the kitchen sink, which is rough and stony and old. Cement shelves protrude from the wall above the sink. Chamdi makes out a sack of rice on one of the shelves. It hangs precariously and he is sure that it will soon fall on the small wooden table below it. A pack of Gold Flake cigarettes lies on the table along with a half-open box of matches. A single tube light flickers on and off, sending strange shocks of light all over Guddi's body. There is little sunlight in this room.

Guddi lies motionless on the floor. Darzi sits on his haunches and presses a white cloth against the wound on her forehead to stop the bleeding. There is some blood on the floor already, but Chamdi knows that it is not from Guddi. It probably belonged to Anand Bhai's brother, Navin. Chamdi wonders where Navin has gone. He was in this room only a short while ago—his moans could be heard.

Darzi might be old, but he sits on his haunches with ease. He has very thin eyebrows and his forehead looks swollen. His white hair is oiled back and it glistens. He gives Chamdi a yellow smile. Chamdi smiles back, but his mind is on the scissors, needle, and thread that are placed on the ground beside Guddi on a piece of white gauze. One hand still on Guddi's wound, Darzi uses the other hand to pull up his checkered lungi. He scratches his right shin. In the heat, he has pulled his white vest halfway up his stomach, which is hairy, just like Anand Bhai's.

"Where's the old woman?" asks Anand Bhai. He takes off his white shirt and wipes his face with it. Then he throws the shirt in a corner. It lands next to a pair of kolhapuri chappals.

"She's put Navin in his room," replies Darzi.

"Is he okay?" asks Anand Bhai.

"In two-three days he'll be fine."

"I'll make those bastards pay."

"I see," says Darzi softly as he lifts the rag off Guddi's forehead. The blood still seeps out. He lets out a *tsk* and places the rag back on her forehead.

"The Muslims have done this," says Anand Bhai. "They will pay."

"What will killing accomplish, Anand?"

"To save a life, you have to take a life. No Hindu is safe until the Muslims are out of this country."

"So now you want to kill any Muslims you can find?"

"I'll start with a few. I'll start with a few Muslim heads. Then I'll show them to Navin—was he the one who bombed the temple? Or was it this one here?"

"What was Navin doing at the temple in the first place? Why was he not at his job?"

"Working for the telephone company is not a job. It is slavery, understand? Anyway I wanted

Navin to meet Namdeo Girhe. Show respect, take his blessings, so that Navin will go up in life."

"Instead Namdeo Girhe went up," says Darzi. "But it would be wise to keep seeking Girhe's blessings."

"What for?"

"Now that he's dead, he has a direct connection with God."

"Joke all you want. The truth is, Bombay will burn now. You watch."

"Even if the Muslims have done this, it's a handful of them," Darzi says. "Why should the rest suffer? We have lived peacefully with Muslims for years. They are our brothers. Only a handful of them have done this. The rest are innocent."

"No one is innocent."

"We almost lost a son today. Don't forget that. And why were you not at the temple? Why send your younger brother?"

Anand Bhai is silent. He looks around the room as though he did not hear Darzi's words. He places his right hand against the doorway and lets out a soft burp. The old woman appears, moves his hand out of her way and enters the room.

"Tell your mother why you did not go to the temple today," says Darzi.

The old woman does not glance at either of them. To Chamdi, she seems much older than Darzi. She looks up at the flickering tube light as if it irritates her.

"Our son was busy getting pleasure from Rani, his whore," says Darzi. "That's why he could not go. But he bravely sent his younger brother instead. His younger brother, who has an honest job."

"Navin will be okay," says the old woman. "I have kept him in his room. He's sleeping. Now tell me, how is Guddi?"

"Yes, will Guddi be okay?" Chamdi asks, brave enough to speak for the first time since he entered Darzi's room.

"Yes," replies Darzi. "But she's weak."

Although Chamdi is relieved to hear this, he knows he has more dangerous matters at hand. He must think of what to tell Anand Bhai about Dabba. And what about Amma—how will he tell her that she has lost her son? Will she even understand what Chamdi is saying? As he thinks about this, his gaze rests on a wooden box in the corner where Anand Bhai threw his shirt. The box has an "Om" on it.

"What are you looking at?" asks the old woman.

"That box," says Chamdi. "It's Guddi's, no?"

"Yes," says the old woman. "She left it here this morning."

Darzi gives a quick nod to the old woman. She walks to the corner with the box and sits down facing the wall. She motions for Chamdi to join her. Chamdi goes to the old woman and sits down beside her. They both have their backs to Darzi, but then Chamdi turns to watch Darzi, who puts a thread through the needle. He reaches for a bottle that contains a colourless liquid. He puts the rag to the mouth of the bottle and wets it a little. He places the cloth over Guddi's nose for a few seconds and then starts stitching her up. That is when Chamdi turns away.

The old woman opens the wooden box. Once again, Chamdi is assaulted by colours, but there is no lift in his heart when he sees the painted gods. Why did the gods not protect Sumdi and Guddi? He thinks of Jesus too and wonders why Jesus let this happen. Perhaps it is best Chamdi left Jesus at the orphanage.

"I make these clay gods," says the old woman. "Guddi sells them for me. She wanted to learn how to make them herself. I hope . . ."

Chamdi notices that the old woman is biting her lip. He turns to look at Guddi, but the old woman puts her hand to his cheek and diverts his attention back to her.

"She will live, no?" asks Chamdi.

"Of course she'll live. With so many gods protecting her, she has to." The old woman smiles. "Look—so many of them—do you know them all, do you know their powers?"

Chamdi shakes his head. The old woman picks a god out of the box. How small the god looks, thinks Chamdi. The old woman should not be holding the god in her palm. It should be the other way round. But he does not say this.

"Do you know who this is?" asks the old woman.

Chamdi shakes his head again.

The god holds a sword in one hand and a lotus in the other. She has two extra arms but they are free—they hold nothing. She is painted yellow and her palms are red.

"That is Durga," says the old woman. "The Invincible One. That means she can never lose. Do you want me to tell you a story about her?"

Chamdi is reminded of Mrs. Sadiq and the *Chandamama* stories she used to tell him.

"No," he says firmly. "I don't like stories."

"Then know this—Durga is protecting our little Guddi. That's why she was saved."

As the old woman tells him this, Chamdi is absent-mindedly scratching his body. The dirt and blood stuck on his oily torso are causing him discomfort.

"What you need more than any god is a bath and some food," says the old woman. "Why don't you go wash up? There's a bathroom."

"No, come with me," says Anand Bhai as he looms in the doorway.

"Let him stay here," pleads the old woman.

"I saved the girl. Now don't interfere."

Anand Bhai's tone is sharp and the old woman does not argue any further. She gently nudges Chamdi on the shoulder. Chamdi gets up and walks to the door. He says a short prayer for Guddi but it is interrupted by Anand Bhai.

"Let's go to my room," says Anand Bhai.

Chamdi squints as he follows Anand Bhai out into the sun again. The adda is secluded now. The goat is still tied to a post and it shakes its head, tries to yank the post out of the ground, to no avail. The green curtain that hangs in the doorway of Anand Bhai's room is still. Anand Bhai's hand rests on Chamdi's shoulder as he leads him past the curtain into his room.

This room is different from Darzi's. Rani lies

on a bed and watches TV. Her hair is tied up in a
bun and she loosens the gold bangles on her wrist
as Chamdi and Anand Bhai enter. She is watching a black-and-white movie.

"Switch it off," says Anand Bhai.

Rani gets up from the bed and does as she is
told. She looks at Anand Bhai, awaits further
instructions.

"Get me some chicken from the Mughlai restaurant. And get it fast. Abdul will have it ready."

As Rani leaves the room, she glances at Chamdi.
But she does not say a word. Chamdi notices that
there are patches of dark blue on her left arm.

"Get pieces that are not oily," Anand Bhai
says.

But Rani has already left the room. The green
curtain is still once again, as though Rani did not
pass through it only seconds ago.

"Do you like oil in your food?" asks Anand
Bhai.

Chamdi is unsure of what to say. He has never
thought about it before. "No," he decides. "I don't
like oil."

"Then why are you carrying it all over your
body?"

Chamdi remains silent.

"Why is your body covered with oil?" asks Anand Bhai.

"I . . . I don't know."

"How can you not know?"

"I was playing . . . we were playing a game, Sumdi and I."

Anand Bhai's grip tightens on Chamdi's shoulder. "What were you trying to steal?"

"Nothing . . ."

"The only time a person smears himself in oil is when he wants to be slippery. What did you want to slip away from?"

Now Chamdi is in pain. Anand Bhai's hand is pressing a nerve on his shoulder, applying more and more pressure. Chamdi looks at the blank TV screen as pain shoots through him. His mouth is half open, ready to let out a yelp, a cry, anything, but instead he slumps to the floor in agony.

"The temple . . ." groans Chamdi.

Anand Bhai lets go. "The temple?"

"It was Sumdi's idea to rob the temple money," says Chamdi.

The moment the words come out of his mouth, he is ashamed for blaming his friend. He hopes

Sumdi will forgive him. He has no choice left
but to tell Anand Bhai the truth.

"I was going to slip in through the side window
of the temple and steal the puja money. Please
forgive me."

"What about Dabba?"

"Dabba is dead. I did not lie about him being
dead."

"The jeweller."

Chamdi does not know what to say. It is best
to stay silent. He does not have the guts to look
Anand Bhai in the face. He stares at the grey,
stony floor.

"I see," says Anand Bhai.

The telephone rings in Anand Bhai's room,
but he does not move. Chamdi still has his head
down and he shivers, fully expecting a massive blow to the head. The ring of the telephone
becomes uncomfortable because Anand Bhai
remains still. The moment the phone stops ringing, Anand Bhai speaks.

"Do you see that drawer?" asks Anand Bhai.

Chamdi still does not look up. Anand Bhai
lightly places his finger under Chamdi's chin
and forces him to look up. Chamdi looks at

Anand Bhai's beard. The two grains of rice are still entangled in the hair. Anand Bhai turns Chamdi's head to the right, in the direction of an old wooden chest of drawers.

"Go open the top drawer," says Anand Bhai.

Chamdi tries to get up but his legs let him down.

"Don't make me say it again," says Anand Bhai.

Chamdi wants to tell Anand Bhai that he does not have the strength to get up, but instead he places his palms on the ground and boosts himself. He walks past the blank TV screen to the drawer.

"Open it," says Anand Bhai.

Chamdi holds the rusted brass handle and pulls.

"You'll find a map in the drawer," says Anand Bhai.

The map is the only thing in the drawer. Chamdi looks at it closely. It is large and folded and there are brown marks on it—like chai stains. The word BOMBAY is printed on it.

"There's something beneath the map," says Anand Bhai.

Chamdi places his hand on the map. He can feel something beneath it. Something hard. He holds one end of the map and lifts it.

A knife. It resembles the butcher's knife Munna stole.

He looks back at Anand Bhai.

"Bring it here."

Chamdi holds the knife by the handle and he does not like the feel of it in his hand. The black handle does not look new—it is smooth with use. He holds it very lightly and makes sure that the tip of the blade faces the ground. He is now only a foot away from Anand Bhai.

"Now cut your tongue off," says Anand Bhai.

Chamdi is sure he has not heard Anand Bhai's words correctly.

"You lied to me," says Anand Bhai. "So hold your tongue out and slice it off."

Anand Bhai's tone is casual. There is no hatred in it. He stands with his arms folded across his hairy chest.

"I'm waiting," says Anand Bhai. "Either you do it, or I'll do it. The problem with me is that I'm a perfectionist. That means I will work slow and steady and make sure that the cut is in one straight line. If not, I'll start again."

"Please, Anand Bhai," begs Chamdi. "I'm sorry. I lied to save Guddi."

"And she has been saved. But you have to pay.

Like Munna. Remember Munna? I caught him with the very knife that you are holding, but I did not harm him until he disrespected me by talking back, when he said that he does not care about the police. Only I abuse the police, no one else. So Munna had to be punished. Same for you because you disrespected me by lying."

"Please . . ."

"Okay," says Anand Bhai. "I'll do it. Give me the knife." He takes the knife from Chamdi's hand. He holds it in his right hand and places his left hand on Chamdi's shoulder.

"Don't worry," he says. "You'll still be able to hear. It's more important to *listen* than speak."

Chamdi tries to move away but Anand Bhai stares him down. Chamdi knows it is foolish to run. By the time he reaches the green curtain, Anand Bhai's knife will have carved part of Chamdi's back.

"Stick your tongue out," says Anand Bhai.

"Please . . ." says Chamdi as he folds his hands and begs.

"Stick your tongue out!"

The snarl in Anand Bhai's voice jolts Chamdi and his tongue slips out of his mouth. Anand Bhai digs his nails into the tip of Chamdi's tongue.

"No wonder you lie so much," he says. "You have a long tongue. Don't move. If you move even one inch, this knife will enter your eye. Now I will cut your tongue in one stroke, not to worry, hah? On the count of three I'll do it. Take a deep breath. One-two . . ."

Chamdi makes strange desperate sounds. With his tongue out it is hard for him to speak.

"Stop making sounds. You're not dumb yet," says Anand Bhai.

He makes a small cut on the edge of Chamdi's tongue. The blood trickles down the blade of the knife.

"Can you feel it?" he asks. "I've started."

Tears form in Chamdi's eyes. Anand Bhai lets go.

"I'm sorry," says Chamdi. "Let me go, I'll . . ."

"You'll what?" asks Anand Bhai. "Talk while you still have a tongue left."

"I'll do anything for you," says Chamdi.

"I asked you to cut your tongue off. Such a simple task, but you can't perform."

"Anything else. I'll beg for you my whole life."

"Beg? Who cares about begging?"

"Whatever you want. I'll steal."

"What else?"

"I'll steal, I'll . . . do whatever you ask."

"Are you sure?"

"I promise," says Chamdi.

Anand Bhai runs his index finger along the blade of the knife. He sniffs hard a couple of times, as though there is something irritating his nostrils. He hands Chamdi the knife.

"Put the knife back in the drawer," says Anand Bhai.

Chamdi walks to the drawer. The cut on his tongue burns. The telephone rings again. Rani enters through the green curtain with a white plastic bag in her hand. The thought of eating makes Chamdi ill. In any case, the cut on his tongue will make eating difficult and painful. Rani sees that Anand Bhai is silent. She places the plastic bag on the TV and answers the phone. She begins talking in a hushed tone as though she senses what has just happened in the room.

"I like you," Anand Bhai tells Chamdi. "You risked your life to save your friend. I need men like that."

Chamdi is confused.

"You are sharp also," continues Anand Bhai. "I believed you about Dabba. But I would have taken that out of you in one second if I wanted. It's just that I have to keep the old woman happy. In her old age she worries too much about me. I saved Guddi for her peace of mind. In the days to come I will be forced to take many lives and God is my witness—I have saved a little girl's life. So that's why I did it. Anyway, I like you."

Chamdi does not understand why Anand Bhai likes him now. Only moments ago, he was about to slice off Chamdi's tongue.

"Let's eat," says Anand Bhai. "Get off the phone, Rani."

Rani nods her head and whispers goodbye into the phone. She places the black receiver back into its cradle.

"Do you like chicken?" Anand Bhai asks Chamdi. "It's Mughlai food. Best in the world. But it's spicy. No matter how much we tell Abdul, he does not listen. Sorry about the cut. It will burn, but you're a tough boy."

Suddenly, Chamdi is afraid again. Anand Bhai seems even more dangerous when he is friendly.

"What are you going to do to me?" asks Chamdi.

"For now, nothing," says Anand Bhai. "For now, we eat."

Chamdi sleeps on the floor of Anand Bhai's room, his knees tucked into his chest. His mouth is slightly open. Each time the cut on his tongue burns, he opens his eyes a little, but he quickly closes them and tries to sleep. He has been floating in and out of sleep for hours now.

"Get up," says Anand Bhai. "Time to go."

Dazed, Chamdi looks around the room. The tube light is on and Anand Bhai's bed is made. Rani is nowhere to be seen. Chamdi glances out the window—it is night.

"Go wash yourself," says Anand Bhai. "I've cleaned the car. Don't want you to stain the seat."

Mutely, Chamdi gets up and walks to the bathroom. He shuts the door and steps over a small parapet that separates the toilet from the bathing area. As he removes his shorts, a bougainvillea petal slips out of his pocket. It looks old. He lets it remain on the floor. He does not remove the cloth from around his neck. Let it get wet. It will keep him cool.

He grabs a white plastic mug that floats on water contained in a steel bucket, dips the mug into the water and opens his mouth wide. He grimaces as the water soothes his cut, then takes another mugful and pours it over his head. This will be his first bath since he left the orphanage. He looks around for soap and sees a light blue soapbox. He does not care to ask Anand Bhai's permission. He scrubs himself until the dust particles and dirt slowly disappear down the drain.

As he does this, Chamdi thinks about Guddi. Darzi and the old woman are good people—they will take care of her, he reassures himself.

Soon, Chamdi is clean. There is no towel in the bathroom, but Chamdi spots an orange napkin on the window ledge and uses it to dry himself. He lets his hair stay wet. He thinks of Guddi in Darzi's room and imagines her walking and laughing. I will enter that room and she will be on her feet, he convinces himself. He puts his shorts back on and steps out of the bathroom. He will have to ask Anand Bhai for a shirt since he no longer has his white vest. He tries not to remember the events that led to the removal of that vest.

"What happened to your ribs?" asks Anand Bhai. "They are like knives."

Chamdi does not respond, though he wants to tell Anand Bhai that they are not ribs, they are tusks, and they will one day be used against the likes of him. Mrs. Sadiq was the only person who did not make him feel conscious of his skinny frame. She always told him that he would gain flesh with age. He is pierced by a sudden longing to be with her.

"Can you please give me a shirt?" asks Chamdi.

"What happened to yours?"

Chamdi remains silent. Anand Bhai goes to the wooden chest of drawers, the one that contains the knife. He opens the bottom drawer, takes out a white T-shirt and throws it at Chamdi.

"I play cricket in that T-shirt," says Anand Bhai. "I love India. Good team, but ma ki chud you cannot depend on them. Some days they are dynamite, some days they are hollow."

Chamdi finds it strange that even though he is so different from Anand Bhai, the two of them enjoy the same game. Chamdi has not seen a single game of street cricket in Bombay like he imagined he would. He has not even seen a red rubber ball.

He puts on the T-shirt. It is so big for him that the sleeves come down almost to his wrists. He tucks it into his shorts and it balloons over the top, but he does not care. He wishes he could get fresh shorts too.

"I want to see Guddi," says Chamdi.

"Now now. She's sleeping."

"But . . ."

"Darzi and the old woman are also resting. We cannot disturb."

Why does Anand Bhai not call Darzi and the old woman Father and Mother? Here is someone who has not one parent but two whole parents, and he never refers to them as Father and Mother.

Anand Bhai waits for Chamdi at the door. The green curtain has been parted to one side. Chamdi wonders how late it is. He can see that most of the doors of the other rooms in the adda are shut. An oil lamp has been placed at the foot of Darzi's door, which is also closed. The small flame of the oil lamp flickers.

As they near the car, Chamdi feels ill. He does not want to sit in the car. Anand Bhai opens the passenger door for him, but Chamdi stalls, looks around the darkness of the adda. At the orphanage, Chamdi had the bougainvilleas to comfort him. Even at night he could use his mind to light them up and any fear or illness he felt was reduced. He wishes he could do the same at the adda, but all he can see are the tomatoes and cucumbers that grow behind Darzi's room. They fail to soothe him.

Anand Bhai taps the inside of the car window. Chamdi gets in but does not look at the back seat. He looks straight ahead and does not say a word. The car starts and the headlights shine on the tomatoes and cucumbers. They look horrified by the light, thinks Chamdi. The redness of the tomatoes reminds him of blood. Why did God make blood and flowers and vegetables the same colour?

The alley behind the adda has no streetlights so only the headlights of the car light the way. There are holes in the road, a few plastic bags are floating along the street, and a man has placed a cot on the footpath. This man uses his shirt as a pillow. Chamdi's eyes shut as the car hits a stretch of road that he does not recognize. He has no interest in his surroundings, and he wants to shut his ears as well because now he can hear Sumdi breathing onto his neck from the back seat. Chamdi turns his head and looks at the back seat—he is imagining things.

"Your friend's in the trunk," says Anand Bhai.

Chamdi shuts his eyes again as the car speeds up. He opens his eyes only when the car slows down and enters a short lane lined by trees on either side. The lane opens out into a large clearing. The car comes to a halt.

Chamdi and Anand Bhai step out of the car, and Chamdi looks up at the night sky. He wonders if Sumdi is already up there or if he is still in his body. But Sumdi was so eager to run that he would not wait in his body if he did not have to.

Anand Bhai opens the trunk of the car. He looks at Chamdi, who understands that he must help Anand Bhai lift the body. Chamdi does not want to see his friend's face. He knows that he will forever hold a picture of Sumdi's face in his brain: teeth slipping out of his mouth and falling onto the cement road.

He is relieved to see that Sumdi's body is covered in a white cloth. Anand Bhai holds one end of the body, and Chamdi the other. With one hand, Anand Bhai quickly slams the trunk shut.

Chamdi sees a number of sheds with tin roofs in the clearing. Below each roof is a cement slab and on the slab are logs for the dead body. There are at least seven to eight fires roaring at the same time. At a tap near the sheds, an old man washes his hands under streaming water. He then uses the bottom of his kurta to wipe his hands and face. Men, dressed mainly in white, gather near the bodies of the dead. The women sit on

benches away from the funeral pyre. A young
woman's wails pierce the dusty air. An older
woman dressed in a cream salwar kameez rubs the
younger woman's back to soothe her, but it seems
to make no difference. The young woman's cries
mix with the sound of crackling wood. A group
of men walk past Chamdi carrying a body on a
stretcher. They do not utter a word and simply
take in the sobs that come from some of the sheds.
The sobs make Chamdi think of just one thing:
how to tell Guddi that her brother is dead. He
knows that she is a brave girl, but how she will
bear the news? What he fears most is that there
will be no crying. What if she simply closes her
eyes and never wakes up again?

Anand Bhai leads Chamdi to one of the sheds
with a funeral pyre, the wood neatly stacked up.
They place the body on the ground. Chamdi does
not want to take the cloth off Sumdi's body.

But Anand Bhai whips it off.

Chamdi forces himself to look. Sumdi's face is
even more destroyed than Chamdi remembers.

A man comes towards them. Chamdi can tell
that the man is a priest because of the red tikka
on his forehead. A young boy, perhaps two or
three years older than Chamdi, follows the priest.

Anand Bhai lifts Sumdi's body and places it over the wood. The logs are arranged very neatly and covered in oil. Chamdi stares at Sumdi's body—it is unclean and bloody. He wonders if he should burn the white cloth with the three drops of blood on it right here, right now, along with Sumdi's body. It is of no use, he tells himself. I am foolish to think that it will lead me to my father. Look at what it has done for me so far.

The priest begins chanting prayers, but Anand Bhai stops him. The priest then sprinkles a liquid over the body. The young boy holds a flaming log in his hand and he looks at Anand Bhai, who turns to Chamdi. The flame is a yellow shiver in the wind. The priest places a few small logs on the body, and Sumdi's face is no longer visible. Chamdi wants to take the logs off, he wants to have one last look, a word perhaps, a whisper in Sumdi's ear. If Sumdi had a choice about going, he would like to go with a beedi in his mouth.

The young boy hands Chamdi the flaming log.

Chamdi wants to say a prayer, but when he tries to think of God or heaven, prayer is replaced by flashes of the gaping hole in the temple.

Chamdi touches the end of the flaming log to Sumdi's feet.

He cannot bear to start with the face.

What angers him is that Anand Bhai is watching Sumdi burn. It should be the other way round.

As Chamdi hears the people at the funeral pyres around him wail, he wonders why he is not crying too. What if Sumdi were to see him right now? Sumdi would be surprised that Chamdi is just as lifeless and unaffected as Anand Bhai is. Chamdi does not know what to do, so he releases the flaming log and watches in silence as the flames travel along Sumdi's body.

Chamdi stands outside the closed door of Darzi's room. The white cloth is no longer around his neck. It is a bundle in his hand. He took it off at the cremation site, and it now contains Sumdi's ashes.

He taps on the door. Anand Bhai had asked him not to, but Chamdi no longer cares. He looks towards Anand Bhai's room. The light is off. Anand Bhai must be asleep by now. Just as Chamdi is about to tap a little harder, the old woman opens the door. She does not say a word as she lets him in.

Darzi is asleep on the ground, snoring loudly. His hands are clasped across his stomach and his

head faces the ceiling. The old woman goes back
to her place beside Darzi. Chamdi asks himself
why Anand Bhai does not give his parents a bed.
But perhaps they prefer to sleep on the hard
floor, just like Mrs. Sadiq.

Chamdi approaches Guddi in the darkness
of the room. He places the white bundle on the
floor. Guddi lies on the floor in a position similar to that of Darzi. Her forehead is bandaged,
and as Chamdi bends down he can hear her
breathe lightly. He wonders again how he will tell
Guddi about Sumdi's death. Maybe she knows
already. What should he say to her? What should
his exact words be?

Your brother is dead.

Sumdi died.

Sumdi did not live.

Sumdi.

Yes, that is all he needs to say. He only needs to
utter her brother's name. She will know.

Chamdi takes Guddi's hand in his, anxious for
her to wake up. He knows it is better if she rests,
but she has to face Sumdi's death as soon as possible, for he cannot bear it alone. Not that he feels
too much. In fact, he is repeatedly surprised at
himself that he feels so little. Sumdi could have

been like a brother to me, he thinks, but that would have taken time.

As Chamdi thinks this, Guddi stirs. Perhaps Guddi has read his mind. Or perhaps Sumdi is talking to her already, telling her that he has finally reached their village, except that it is slightly different than expected, but it is their village no doubt because he recognizes some of the other people around, and, of course, he knows the village head as well, and he will soon meet him, but he has no fear, for he has lived as clean a life as the streets of Bombay allowed him and he is sure that the village head will understand.

Chamdi places his hand on Guddi's forehead. She looks at him and says nothing, and three thoughts flash through his brain: *I hope she is not blind. I hope she is not deaf. I hope she has not lost her voice.* Any of these could be possible, he knows, because he has been spared completely and one person always bears an unfair burden.

But Guddi looks into his eyes and Chamdi's first doubt is cleared. He wants to say something so that she can respond and the second and third fears can vanish as well, but he does not know what to say. He could tell her it was a bomb, or that the politician died, or that Anand Bhai has promised there will be more riots—he could tell her all this, but she would not care at all.

And that is when Guddi opens her mouth and says softly, "Sumdi."

Now Chamdi knows that he does not need to explain a thing because his hand betrays him as it clutches Guddi's tightly. The sick feeling of a while ago returns to him like the very heat of the flames. He can feel the flames all over him, especially on his face, and he is ashamed of how he is shaking while Guddi is completely still, staring at him for what seems to be a long time, and then she trembles, her grip on his hand tightens, as though a bomb of pain has exploded in her as well.

In the early morning, Chamdi and Guddi walk to Grant Road Bridge. Even though Guddi was too weak to leave the house, Chamdi explained that they needed to fulfill Sumdi's dream. That was all he said.

As they climb up the steps that lead to the bridge, Chamdi can sense that Guddi is worried about Amma—he went back to the kholi to fetch her, but she was not there. He imagines Amma wandering aimlessly through the streets with a baby in her arms, not knowing that her son is dead.

Chamdi remembers the night he and Guddi rode in the horse carriage. It was the only time he experienced happiness, and he is grateful for that feeling. His mind returns to the white bundle that he holds in his hand. How strange life is, he thinks. I was once wrapped in this white cloth, and now my friend is in it.

They climb the final step and onto the bridge itself. Guddi leans on Chamdi for support. The walk, even though it was very short, has tired her. It is still early so the bridge is clear, but a few street hawkers are setting up their temporary stalls near the entrance to the railway station. A man who sells lime juice washes his glasses. A man who sells combs, mirrors, and small diaries places a blue plastic sheet on the ground and arranges his wares, as do two women who sell travel bags and clothes.

Guddi is shaking with fever. A striped shawl covers her dress. The old woman gave it to Guddi to prevent her from shivering. Darzi said fever was to be expected because of the stitches. It was nothing to worry about.

Railway commuters cross the street and wait for an oncoming bus. A local train rumbles below the bridge, and Chamdi sees a few faces peering out of the windows of the buildings along the railway tracks. Crows perch on the electric lines above the tracks.

Chamdi and Guddi stand in the middle of the bridge, against a dark stone wall. A man relieves himself on the wall, but he zips up quickly and crosses the street. Chamdi looks down at the tracks. A small boy places an empty coconut shell on the tracks and waits for the train to crush it. A little farther ahead, a man staggers alongside the tracks, clutching a bottle. The sound of the train fades, clears the way for Chamdi's words. But Guddi speaks first.

"I can't stand for long," she says. "I'm feeling very weak."

"I know," he replies softly.

Chamdi places the white bundle on the railing of the bridge.

"Do you know what your brother dreamt of?" he asks.

"Many things," she says. "We both dreamt of going to our village."

"What else? What was his secret wish?"

"I don't know," she says. "I'm very tired."

"Your brother wanted to fly. He said that his leg made him heavy and it was his dream to fly. That's why we are here."

Chamdi carefully opens the knot of the white cloth.

"I can't believe that's him," says Chamdi at last.

Guddi simply stares at the ashes. The sun casts light on the surrounding buildings and makes them seem less desolate. In the distance, the high-rises of Bombay loom over the city and stare down at its slums.

"I want to say this and I don't know how," says Chamdi. "But I loved your brother even though I knew him for only three days."

"I loved him too. So did Amma."

"I hope we can find Amma," Chamdi says. "She's not at the kholi. I hope she comes back."

Guddi looks at the tracks, and Chamdi can tell from the tremble of her lips that she is trying hard not to cry.

"We must help him fly," Chamdi tells her.

They carefully lift Sumdi together, release him over the bridge and into the sky.

Sumdi breaks into a thousand different parts, bits of grey that shine in the sunlight as they soar over the railway tracks. Chamdi thinks of the ashes as tiny birds, each bearing a particular trace of Sumdi: his smile, his jagged teeth, his foul mouth, his deep scar, his polio leg, his arm around Chamdi's shoulder, his laughter in his sister's ear.

As the last of the ashes leave the white cloth, Chamdi lets go of the cloth itself.

Go land at my father's feet, he says to the cloth. The three drops of blood will help him recognize the cloth. Now it is his turn to find me.

Chamdi wishes Mrs. Sadiq were here to witness this moment because she would have been very proud of him. Her words come to him: *You are no longer ten. You are a man now and it is my fault that I have made you the man you are.* But Chamdi is grateful to her. He wants her to know that.

In a way, it is okay if my father is dead, he thinks. If I miss my father without even knowing him, thinks Chamdi, I can imagine how hard the separation must be for my mother. If they are both dead, at least they are together.

And soon, he tells himself, Sumdi will fly over the city and visit the Bombay he loved—every dirty corner. He will watch cricket matches and cock fights, he will enter gambling dens and play till his pockets are empty and his heart full. Some parts of him will fall on the roof of that local train, where he will remain until the train reaches the end of the line, but some parts of him will continue to fly, they will circle the city and then the world, and it will not be the world Chamdi knows. It will be a world seen from the sky.

Chamdi looks at Guddi, who is crying, and suddenly he knows exactly what he must say to her. "*Khile Soma Kafusal*," says Chamdi as he caresses Guddi's face. "I speak to you in the Language of Gardens."

This time, Guddi does not ask what his words mean because the way he looks at her tells her the exact meaning. But clearly, Chamdi's words are not enough.

"Sumdi is free," Guddi says. "But we are stuck here."

"No, we are not," says Chamdi.

"We'll never be able to leave Bombay."

"That's fine," he says. "Because Bombay will leave us."

"What do you mean?"

"Kahunsha will be born."

"Is such a thing possible?" asks Guddi, hopefully.

"If you can think it, it's possible," says Chamdi.

TWELVE

The old woman brings two steaming glasses of tea. Anand Bhai and Chamdi sit on the steps out-side Darzi's room. Chamdi notices that there are three steps, the same number as at the orphanage. How he loved walking down those steps and being greeted by the bougainvilleas. Anand Bhai's adda lacks colour. Perhaps it is not possible for plants and flowers to grow in the presence of such a human being.

Darzi gave Guddi a pill for the pain and she is asleep again. Chamdi liked the way Darzi read out the name of the white pill—*Comb-bee-flaam*—as though it were a magic seed. He wishes he had parents like Darzi and the old woman. He would use Father and Mother because those are words he has never been able to say in his life.

Anand Bhai sips his tea and stares at the wall that separates his adda from the school. Two sparrows peck at the ground in front of them.

"Drink your tea," says Anand Bhai.

"It's very hot," says Chamdi. "The cut on my tongue burns."

Anand Bhai places the glass of tea down and puts his arm around Chamdi.

Chamdi is uncomfortable—Anand Bhai's touch is not warm. Mrs. Sadiq was the only person whose touch comforted Chamdi, but he never let her know that.

"Do you know what injustice is?" asks Anand Bhai.

"I . . . yes."

"Explain to me."

"If someone good suffers, then it's wrong. Like that?"

Anand Bhai takes his hand off Chamdi's shoulder. He removes a packet of Gold Flake cigarettes from the pocket of his white shirt. He taps the cigarette three times on the pack. Chamdi asks himself what Anand Bhai is thinking about—

perhaps his own childhood, when he ran around the adda and played cricket with boys his age. It is hard for Chamdi to imagine that Anand Bhai was once a child. Anand Bhai lights the cigarette with his gold lighter and lets out streaks of smoke through his lips.

"Do you remember what I told you about Radhabai Chawl?"

"Yes," says Chamdi.

But Anand Bhai continues as though he did not want his question to be answered.

"It was a burning of innocents, a grave *injustice*. Do you understand? Also, what happened at the temple . . . your friend Sumdi. There was no need for him to die. Even my brother Navin got hurt."

"Yes . . ." says Chamdi. "But there's nothing we can do."

Anand Bhai takes a deep drag from his cigarette and bares his teeth to Chamdi. As he exhales, the sparrows that were picking on food crumbs fly right above his head.

"There *is* something we can do," he says. "We must let the Muslims know that God is on our side, not theirs."

The mention of God once again reminds Chamdi of the gaping hole in the temple, of

Ganesha's trunk lying helpless on the street, unable to rise and spray water on the flames. Chamdi has seen the gods that the old woman makes too and they are so small, they fit in a wooden box. He has seen Jesus, who is life-sized, but even Jesus is powerless.

"What do you think?" asks Anand Bhai.

"I . . . about what?"

"What do you think we should do?"

"I don't know," says Chamdi. "Nothing."

"Nothing? Your friend died and you want to just sit there? You don't want revenge? If anyone harms my Hindu brothers, I will rip that person to shreds."

Anand Bhai flicks his cigarette to the ground. Chamdi looks at the sparking butt of the cigarette.

"We will replicate Radhabai Chawl for the Muslims," says Anand Bhai. "And it will happen in many parts of the city at the same time, not only here."

Chamdi does not understand exactly what Anand Bhai means. Anand Bhai scratches his chest, grits his teeth as he does this.

"You will come along. Be part of our gang. It will be training for you. I want my men to see you, that even though you are so small you are not scared in the face of danger. They will be impressed. That's how you earn your place in the gang. The future is in you young boys. If I have fifty Chamdis, then think of how much power I will have in a few years."

"But . . ."

"You will do as I say, Chamdi. You work for me now," says Anand Bhai.

Anand Bhai stands up and throws away the tea that remains in his glass. It lands on the gravel. He smoothes his beard and looks down at the map the spilt tea has made.

"I own you," says Anand Bhai. "Remember that."

Chamdi does not know what to do. He understands now why Mrs. Sadiq was so against the children going out into the city, why she wanted everyone to leave Bombay.

More than ever, he yearns for Mrs. Sadiq, for her long, bony hands.

THIRTEEN.

It is very late at night. Even though all the doors
and windows of the one-room homes are closed,
Anand Bhai's adda is busy. About fifteen men
have gathered, and Chamdi watches as some of
them smoke cigarettes, others stretch their limbs,
and a couple pace about outside Anand Bhai's
room. Most of the men are short and thin. They
are dressed plainly: dark shirts, jeans or trousers,
and chappals. Munna is present too. Munna has a
white bandage around his eye. He too shall carry
Anand Bhai's signature for the rest of his life.
Chamdi looks for Jackpot and Handsome, but
they are nowhere to be seen. It makes sense—they

are of no use tonight. Chamdi feels Munna's stern gaze upon him as if Munna does not approve of Chamdi being here.

Tonight, Anand Bhai wears a black shirt instead of his usual white shirt. His trousers are black too. It is like a uniform. Anand Bhai holds a large piece of folded paper and a flashlight in his left hand as he walks towards his men. He greets each man individually and Chamdi hears some of their names: Rathore, Vishnu, and Sitaram.

Anand Bhai walks to the car, which is parked at the back of the adda outside Darzi's room, near the tomatoes and cucumbers. Anand Bhai gets in and drives the car to the centre of the adda where the men have gathered. The headlights shine on the walls of the one-room homes and make the cracks stand out.

Anand Bhai gets out of the car and opens the trunk. As it swings up, Chamdi remembers Sumdi, lifeless under the white cloth. Anand Bhai uses a flashlight to display the contents of the trunk. There are knives, like the one Anand Bhai used on Chamdi's tongue, there are long curving swords, their handles in bad condition, and there is a solid iron rod. There is also a large padlock, the kind Chamdi has seen on shop shutters. And there are two cricket bats.

Anand Bhai faces his men and speaks in a strong voice.

"This city has become dangerous," he says. "The Muslims are warriors too, just like us. That much I will give them. They are also tigers. But the rule is that every jungle must have only one tiger. And in an Indian jungle, there is place for a Hindu tiger only. I appreciate that you are all doing your duty as Hindus. Now pick your weapons. Except Munna and Chamdi."

Hands reach out and grab knives and swords. There is the clink of blades as the weapons graze each other. When all the knives and swords are gone, a man picks the iron rod. He feels its surface and kisses it.

"Come on," says Anand Bhai. "No cricketers here? These bats have smashed a few heads. Take the bats. Let's enjoy some night cricket."

Two men reach for the bats. Their blades are thick and the wood looks old but solid. The rubber around the wooden handles is used, yet intact.

"What about me?" asks Munna.

"You get the iron lock," says Anand Bhai. "You get to lock the family in."

Munna reaches into the corner of the trunk and lifts the iron lock.

"Don't shut it," says Anand Bhai. "I don't have a key."

"Yes, Anand Bhai," replies Munna. His tongue comes out of his mouth a little, as if he is holding food that he likes.

Anand Bhai slams the trunk shut. Chamdi is relieved that he has not been asked to pick a weapon. Perhaps all Anand Bhai wants him to do is watch. Anand Bhai places a large folded piece of paper on the trunk of the car. Chamdi sees it is the map of Bombay that was in Anand Bhai's drawer. Anand Bhai unfolds the map and shines the flashlight on it. Even though Chamdi is scared, the map fascinates him. He has never seen Bombay before. It has such an odd shape, and from where Chamdi stands it seems as though Bombay has a huge mouth, the yawn of a terrible *Chandamama* creature. There are lines along its body and he guesses they are roads, but he cannot help but think of them as cracks in the creature's skin. It looks as if Bombay is cut and bruised.

"There will be multiple strikes," says Anand Bhai. "That is what I have been told."

"By whom?" asks the man with the iron rod.

"The order has come from top. That's all I can say. As we speak, something is happening in Byculla."

Anand Bhai's forefinger points to Byculla on the map. It is deep in the throat of the creature, only a few inches away from its screaming mouth.

"Tonight, there will be trouble in Byculla, Parel, and Dadar," says Anand Bhai. "I know that none of you need this map, you all know the city well, but I brought it here for a reason. See the name on the map. What does it say?"

"Bombay," comes the answer.

"From now on, we are never to utter that name again. This island belongs to the goddess Mumbadevi, and we must reclaim it as a Hindu city. Jai Maharashtra!"

Chamdi recognizes the name Maharashtra as the state that Bombay is in. Mrs. Sadiq taught him that. Anand Bhai uses his gold lighter to set the map on fire. "We will cremate Bombay so that Mumbai can be born."

There is silence amongst the men.

"We will leave the Muslim areas alone tonight until we have more men," warns Anand Bhai. "For now, there will be no attacks near Dongri, Madanpura, Agripada, J.J. Hospital, Bhendi

Bazaar. Tonight, we shall start with one family. And before we go, I want to introduce someone."

Anand Bhai shines the flashlight on Chamdi's face, directly into his eyes. Chamdi raises his hand to prevent the glare from hurting him.

"This is Chamdi," says Anand Bhai. "He's my boy. He'll be joining us tonight. It's his initiation in our gang."

"This chintu?" asks someone.

"He may be small, but he has guts," says Anand Bhai. "His friend Sumdi was killed in the blast that killed Namdeo Girhe. Now Chamdi wants to avenge his friend's death. He wants Muslim blood."

Munna looks shocked when he hears this. Chamdi wonders if it is because Munna was not aware of Sumdi's death, or if it is because Anand Bhai has asked Chamdi to be part of the gang. Either way, it does not matter.

"There's a Muslim family in Shaan Gulley. You know Abdul who owns Café Arabia, the Mughlai restaurant round the corner?"

"Spicy chicken Abdul," says the man with the iron rod.

"Yes, that Abdul. His nephew lives in Shaan Gulley."

"Hanif—the taxiwala?"

"Hah, Hanif the taxiwala. He lives with his wife and newborn child. Tonight, we will cremate the three of them at home. Without prayers."

Chamdi's heart stops when he hears this.

Then a thought strikes: What if this is also a trick, like when Anand Bhai made a cut on Chamdi's tongue to teach him a lesson? Anand Bhai might let me go if I tell him I have learned my lesson, thinks Chamdi. Anand Bhai cannot expect me to watch something so terrible.

The man with the iron rod speaks: "I don't see any petrol here."

"It will be made available on site," says Anand Bhai.

"Shaan Gulley is a Hindu area. Why are we so heavily armed to burn down one family?"

"If any of our Hindu brothers have sympathy for Hanif, then our weapons will remind them that duty comes before friendship. The family is well liked in the mohalla—Hanif's wife teaches children how to read and write, and whenever there's an emergency, Hanif lets his neighbours use his taxi free of charge."

The door of Darzi's room opens and the old woman staggers out and stares at the assembled group. Some of the men greet her respectfully, but from afar. No one goes towards her. Chamdi looks at the old woman and wishes with all his heart that she will call him in. He knows that if he runs to her, Anand Bhai will be livid. So he closes his eyes and thinks of the small wooden box that contains the old woman's gods. He begs all the gods to help him.

He cannot believe it when the old woman responds: "Anand, send the boy back in."

Anand Bhai does not answer her. He turns to his men and says, "Let's go."

"How are we going there?" someone asks.

"Luxury bus," says Anand Bhai.

The men laugh as they stride in the direction of the cucumbers and tomatoes.

"Anand," the old woman says again. "Let the boy in. Please."

"Old woman, go back in," he fires.

Darzi emerges from the darkness of the room behind the old woman and places his hands on her shoulders. He leads her back in.

"Anand Bhai," says Chamdi softly, careful to ensure that his words do not reach the ears of any of Anand Bhai's men. "I have learned my lesson. I will never lie again. Please forgive me."

"I forgave long back. This is business. One day, you will be feared and respected just like I am.

I see the future in you. You are brave and your heart is good. Don't worry, even I felt like this the first time I did something daring. But the sick feeling from the heart goes away, you become free. You kill someone, you eat a hot meal, you take a hot woman, and you go to sleep."

"But Anand Bhai . . ."

"It's your duty," says Anand Bhai. "If you don't do your duty, something might happen to Guddi. You don't want Guddi to be harmed, do you?"

It is quiet in the narrow lane that is Shaan Gulley, except for a faint song that crackles on a radio somewhere. The lights are off in each small shack. Big barrels sit outside most of the shacks, and Chamdi can see that these barrels contain water. Some of the rooms are made from wooden planks and bamboo poles, and they have thatched floors, while others look more solid. Some of the kholis are painted green, and clothes and towels hang from small windowsills.

Anand Bhai's men take swift steps and carry swords, knives, and cricket bats. None of the men seem to care that they might be spotted. Anand Bhai has his hand on Chamdi's shoulder. Munna's

fierce stare is upon Chamdi again. Chamdi tucks
his T-shirt deep into his shorts.

The moon shines on the tin roofs of the homes
and catches the blades of the knives and swords.
Chamdi wonders if he should run and warn Hanif's
family that they are going to be attacked. He is a fast
runner, and of what use are his feet if he does not
use them well? But he does not know where Hanif
lives, and even if he did and were to run to Hanif
and warn him, Anand Bhai would harm Guddi.

The gang soon arrives at a dead end. They stop,
facing a larger shack, painted blue, which stands
apart from the rest of the shacks. Small plants
grow from clay pots placed next to the door. A
plastic Bisleri bottle sprouts a withered creeper.
The closed door looks heavy, unlike the doors of
most of the shacks. There is a window, its wooden
shutters closed. A black cycle rests against the
wall, both its tires flat. Beside the blue shack is a
black-and-yellow taxi with a silver carrier on top.
Chamdi wishes that Hanif the taxiwala would
wake up and drive away from this place.

Anand Bhai raises his right hand and his men
stop.

He goes to the shack on his right and taps
lightly on the door. A bare-chested man in a

white lungi opens the door and hands Anand Bhai a large plastic can. It is three-quarters full of liquid. Chamdi assumes it contains petrol. Anand Bhai motions to one of his men to collect it. The man in the lungi hands out one more plastic can. Finally, he gives Anand Bhai a brown bottle. A white rag droops over the mouth of the bottle. There is liquid in this bottle too. The man in the lungi slips back into his shack and quietly shuts the door. Chamdi is confused. How can this man harm his own neighbour?

"Two of you go to the back," whispers Anand Bhai. "There's no door, but there is a small window. No one should escape."

Two men scamper to the back of the blue shack.

Anand Bhai issues orders to two other men. "Pour petrol on the walls, but be careful. We don't want to burn the whole mohalla."

The two men take one can each and start pouring petrol on the side walls. Some of the petrol falls on their jeans and chappals.

"Munna," says Anand Bhai. "Lock up."

Munna stealthily makes his way to the door. He slides the latch closed and then hooks the iron padlock in. He does not bind the lock yet. Perhaps it will make noise and wake Hanif.

"Do you know why I chose this house?" whispers Anand Bhai to Chamdi.

"It's a Muslim house . . . that's why," answers Chamdi, feebly.

"That's the main reason," says Anand Bhai. "But remember this: To truly enjoy your work, there has to be more than one reason. A *bonus*. You see, my childhood sweetheart lives here. Her name is Farhana. She was in love with me and I was in love with her. But she's Muslim. Even though she was mine, she married Hanif. Tonight I get my revenge on the man who stole her. It makes our work extra special."

As Chamdi looks at the small army that surrounds him, he thinks of Mrs. Sadiq, who was not his mother, but who at least was a good human being. He thinks of Pushpa, and how they could have been friends once she grew up. Even Chamdi's father, who ran from Chamdi, seems so much better than Anand Bhai.

Suddenly, an old woman opens the door from one of the small rooms to their left and peers into the darkness.

"Who's there?" she asks.

"Go back in," says Anand Bhai.

The old woman does not listen. She notices the

shadows of men as they pour petrol over the blue shack. Perhaps she sees knife blades. She screams for help at the top of her voice.

"Bolt the doors!" shouts Anand Bhai.

His voice cracks the night open.

The man with the iron rod runs, along with four other men, to the door of the blue shack. Munna locks up.

A light comes on in the blue shack.

Shaan Gulley is awake, but none of Anand Bhai's men panic. Anand Bhai uses his flashlight again. He shines it on the old woman's face. Then he moves it along to scan the rest of the residents of Shaan Gulley. Men, some in trousers, some in khaki shorts, others in checkered lungis, wipe sleep from their eyes, only to be greeted by Anand Bhai's words: "If anyone interferes, they will be killed."

Hanif and his family have realized they are locked in. They bang desperately on the door. Some of the residents step off their thatched floors and onto the lane, only to face swords.

"Go back in," says Anand Bhai.

"What the hell is going on?" asks one of the residents.

Anand Bhai shines the flashlight on his own face. He lights his face from below, and his black beard acquires sparks of gold. The dark circles under his eyes are more prominent than ever.

"Most of you know who I am," he says. "So you will know my intentions are good. Two nights ago, a Hindu family was burned down in Radhabai Chawl in Jogeshwari. We are here to provide justice. Now a Muslim family will burn too. If anyone interferes, they will be killed. So you decide what your own life is worth. In the coming days, the whole city will burn, and this area will need my protection."

"But our homes will also catch fire," says someone.

"The blue house is isolated. We have chosen carefully. Now go back in!"

Anand Bhai's men stand on either side of him. Even though most of them are small and thin, the weapons give them ferocity. The residents retreat to their thatched floors and tin roofs. Anand Bhai lets his flashlight fall to the ground.

The man with the iron rod suddenly steps towards the window of the blue shack, as though he has just heard something.

The window of the blue shack opens.

Without warning, the man rams the iron rod into the face that peers through the window.

There is a sickening crunch and the face disappears. That must be Hanif the taxiwala, thinks Chamdi. The man stands guard outside the window, the iron rod by his side. He looks ready to repeat his actions should the need arise.

In the darkness of the lane, Chamdi can hear a woman scream from inside the blue shack: "Save us, somebody save us!"

He can also hear the wail of a child. It must be Hanif's newborn. Chamdi imagines Hanif lying on the ground, his teeth smashed with an iron rod, blood streaming from his nose and mouth, while his wife bangs on the bolted door with her fists.

Chamdi is unable to move. None of the neighbours come to the family's rescue. Most of the men and women return to their shacks, and the few that remain outside look just as terrified as Chamdi.

Brown bottle in hand, Anand Bhai towers above Chamdi. "Do you know what this is?" he asks. "This is a petrol bomb. You see this white thing—that's the fuse. Once I light the fuse, I want you to throw the bottle in through the window."

Chamdi cannot believe his ears. He just stares at Anand Bhai.

Anand Bhai bends down towards Chamdi: "I want *you* to throw the bomb. That's the only way to make a name for yourself."

"Please . . ." says Chamdi.

"Now burn this family. Or I'll burn you with them."

"Please . . . I can't hurt anyone . . ."

Anand Bhai places his hand around Chamdi's neck and looks straight into his eyes. Even though Chamdi wants to, he is unable to look anywhere else. He gets a sick feeling in the pit of his stomach, as though something wants to come out. Anand Bhai's thumb presses against Chamdi's throat.

"What about Guddi?" asks Anand Bhai. "Think of Guddi."

"You can kill both Guddi and me . . ." says Chamdi. "I can't do this . . ."

"I'll kill you, but not Guddi," says Anand Bhai. "Hanif and his family are going to die anyway, whether you throw this bomb or not. But Guddi's fate is in your hands. Because if you don't throw this bomb, I will sell her. I will sell Guddi to older men."

The words nail into Chamdi. The sick feeling in his stomach gets stronger.

Anand Bhai grips Chamdi's shoulder and pushes him towards the window. The bottle is still in Anand Bhai's other hand.

"Walk to the window," he says. "You are about to become a man."

But Chamdi can barely move.

He hears the scream of a woman. Even though no one is at the window, Chamdi sees her: Hanif's wife with her large black eyes, the same eyes that Chamdi dreamt his mother had.

Anand Bhai thrusts the brown bottle into Chamdi's hands. Anand Bhai keeps his hand around the bottle.

"Please . . ." says Chamdi. "I can't do this . . ."

"Night after night Guddi will cry, she will beg for her life to end and it will be your fault. It's better to throw the bottle. These people are going to die anyway. Think of Guddi. She will be like Khilowna. Do you remember Khilowna?"

Chamdi remembers Khilowna. He remembers the blood.

Anand Bhai takes his hand off the bottle.

He flicks open his gold lighter. The flame flickers.

"I beg you . . ." says Chamdi. "I beg you . . ."

"Do it now, Chamdi. Otherwise I will make

one of my men take her tonight. Guddi will be sold *tonight*."

Chamdi's grip around the bottle tightens.

Anand Bhai lights the fuse. "Throw it!" he commands.

Chamdi flinches as though he is being shot.

He hurls the bottle through the window.

He turns away as the bottle smashes on the floor. Flames rise. Screams shatter the night. It is as though the fire is an animal and it is hungry for humans.

As the men around him flee, Chamdi stares at Anand Bhai, who stands rooted to the ground. Dressed in black, Anand Bhai looks like he is part of the night itself. Chamdi cannot understand how Anand Bhai can smile at a time like this. Anand Bhai shows no intention of running away.

But Chamdi runs.

FOURTEEN

The adda is completely deserted. Not one of
Anand Bhai's men is around. Even the door to his
room is closed. The goat is awake in a corner of
the adda, tied to a wooden post. It lies on its fours
and lifts its head from time to time. Chamdi sits
on the ground and stares at the goat. It has been
more than an hour since he got here, but he has
still not knocked on Darzi's door.

One look at him and Guddi will know that he
has done something terrible. What can he say to
her—that I, Chamdi, have taken lives? Perhaps she
will not recognize him. What if his face has already
begun to change because of what he has just done?

But Mrs. Sadiq would recognize him in a second. He can feel her breath in his ear right now: Remember, once a thief, always a thief. *I am much more than a thief,* he says to her. It would cause her so much pain she would stop breathing altogether.

If only he had stayed at the orphanage. He would have lived with his bougainvilleas all day and night. He closes his eyes and envisions them caressing his face. But the moment they touch him, they recoil.

He sees Hanif's wife instead. She just looks at him, her long black hair in flames.

A sudden scream explodes in the night. Chamdi opens his eyes, but no one is around. He hopes Anand Bhai will cut off his ears, because if his ears remain, they will carry the screams of Hanif and his family for the rest of his life.

Perhaps the people of the mohalla are fighting the fire, he tells himself. The shack will be destroyed, but the family might survive.

As soon as he thinks this, he knows it is impossible. Anand Bhai stayed there to ensure that no one escapes. All Chamdi can hope for is that Hanif's family stops breathing long before the fire does.

He hears a heavy cough through the door. The door opens suddenly—it is the old woman. She is still coughing. She steps out into the night, spits onto the gravel of the adda, and lets out a small "aah." She has still not seen Chamdi. He is not yet ready to face anyone. The old woman turns to re-enter her room.

"Chamdi?" she asks.

Her eyes become narrower as she peers through the darkness. Chamdi does not answer, nor does he stand up. He stays motionless on the floor with his back against the wall—one leg folded, the other outstretched.

"Chamdi . . ." says the old woman again. Her voice is softer this time.

Even though her back is bent already, the old woman bends lower, towards him. Her closeness makes him uncomfortable. She places her palm on his head, keeps it there for a while. She says nothing. She straightens up as much as her body allows and goes back into the room.

He can hear her walk about the room. There is the clash of utensils, followed by Darzi's heavy snoring. It starts and stops abruptly. Chamdi is glad that Guddi is still asleep. He does not have the courage to face her. He decides to get away from the room. Sitting here, he feels cold, like his heart is shivering.

Just as he is about to place his palms on the ground and thrust himself up, he hears a voice: "Tonight, we will enjoy . . ."

It is Anand Bhai. He has a whisky bottle in his left hand and his right hand is around a man's shoulder. It is the man who rammed the iron rod into Hanif's face.

"Rani's bringing a friend," says Anand Bhai. "We'll enjoy. Do you want to enjoy?"

"Yes," says the man. "I want to enjoy."

They both laugh in a hoarse manner, and Chamdi stays extremely still. He hopes they do not notice him. As they are about to walk past him, the door to Darzi's room rattles. A hand pushes the door open and the door hits the wall. Chamdi knows it is Guddi's hand and he wants her to go back in.

Anand Bhai and the man turn in alarm. But the moment they see Guddi standing in the doorway, they relax. Anand Bhai's attention turns to his right, to where Chamdi is crouched.

"Chamdi," says Anand Bhai.

He climbs up the three small steps that lead to Darzi's room and bends down towards Chamdi, just as the old woman did.

"You did well tonight," says Anand Bhai. "You were very brave." He puts his hand on Chamdi's shoulder and squeezes it. "Remember this night. Tonight, you've become a man." Chamdi can smell the alcohol on Anand Bhai's breath. His black shirt sticks to his sweaty chest. Anand Bhai turns to Guddi and asks, "Do you know what our hero did tonight?"

Chamdi is so still, it is as though he has forgotten how to move.

But Anand Bhai moves. He moves towards Guddi. He places his hand on Guddi's head and looks at Chamdi. "The two of you are very special to me," says Anand Bhai. Then he puts his fingers underneath her chin, looks directly at her, and says, "Even you are special, Guddi."

Anger rises from Chamdi's chest. It makes him stand up and face Anand Bhai. His right palm clenches into a fist.

"Remember what I said, Chamdi," says Anand Bhai. "So you be loyal . . ."

The old woman walks out then. She slowly stretches her arm out for Guddi, and Guddi goes close to her and sticks to her body.

"Anand, it's late," she says firmly. "Go to sleep."

When Chamdi notices how Guddi sticks to the old woman's body, he understands something.

Perhaps this is the only place where Guddi is safe. Right here, at Anand Bhai's adda. Right next to Anand Bhai's mother. She cares for Guddi and will not allow Anand Bhai to harm her. Chamdi can never trust Anand Bhai—he can go back on his word in a second—but he can count on the old woman. As long as she is alive, Guddi will be safe. If he and Guddi run, the old woman will not be able to protect them. Anand Bhai will find them and Guddi will suffer terribly.

Anand Bhai puts his hand in the pocket of his black trousers and takes out a fifty-rupee note. He places the money in Chamdi's palm.

"You did well tonight," Anand Bhai says again.

Chamdi cannot bring himself to fold his fingers around the money.

Anand Bhai smiles at the old woman as he climbs down the three steps and takes a swig from the bottle. He places his arm around the man's shoulder again, and they walk towards Anand Bhai's room, their feet crunching the gravel beneath.

Chamdi stares at the money in his hand. It is a fresh fifty-rupee note, more money than he has held in his life. But he despises the touch of it against his skin. He fights the urge to tear it up.

He closes his fingers over the note and puts it into the pocket of his shorts. He will need money now. He will need it to feed Guddi and Amma. He might need it to run. He does not know.

The old woman enters the room again. He can hear her pouring water into a vessel. His legs feel weak and he sits down once more. Guddi sits down too. She does not say anything. Chamdi watches Anand Bhai open the door of his room. He puts the whisky bottle to his mouth, finishes whatever is left, and throws the empty bottle to the ground.

Chamdi stares at the wall that separates the adda from the school playground. In a few hours, the sun will rise. The doors of the one-room homes will open, the smell of beedis will flood the adda, and the school bell will ring.

Chamdi can feel Guddi looking at him. He continues to stare at the cement wall in front of him.

"What happened?" she asks softly.

Chamdi wants to close his eyes and place his head in Guddi's lap, but he is unable to. An eerie silence envelops the adda as if everyone is awake in the darkness.

FIFTEEN

Slabs of stone are visible amongst the ruins of the burnt building. Rats dive into holes as bits of glass sparkle under the streetlights.

Guddi walks in front of Chamdi with three bananas in her hand. The old woman gave them to her and asked them to come back for chapattis and dal the next day. She also said she would let Guddi have a bath if she wished.

As they approach their kholi, Guddi increases the pace of her steps.

Amma is back at the kholi. She holds the baby in her arms, looks to the night sky, and whispers as though she is offering her own child to the sky for safekeeping.

Guddi goes towards Amma and gently places her palm on Amma's back. Amma keeps looking at the sky, but hands the baby to Guddi, then stops whispering. She shakes her head from side to side as she slowly lowers her gaze.

Guddi places the baby on a plastic sheet beneath the kholi. She peels a banana and feeds it to Amma. Amma holds on to Guddi's hand—she does not want Guddi to let go of the banana. She swallows it down, like it is liquid. Chamdi wonders if the baby is still unwell. When morning comes, he will buy some milk for it. He will see to it that the baby does not die.

He spots something on the ground in a corner of the kholi. A lump forms in his throat as he holds Sumdi's cream shirt in his hand. It smells of sweat and beedis. It must have been the last thing Sumdi touched. He must have thrown his shirt to the ground just before he positioned himself outside the temple. Chamdi wonders how a shirt can make him feel like this. He did not cry even once when the fire was burning Sumdi's body, but now this shirt . . .

Amma finishes the banana and lies down next

to the baby and closes her eyes. She does not even know she has lost a son, thinks Chamdi. A couple of flies sit on her face and he drives them away. She licks her lips as he does this. He wipes off droplets of sweat from the baby's stomach, but quickly takes his hand off it.

Now Guddi eats a banana, and she hands Chamdi the one that remains. He begins to peel it, but he does so very slowly, as though he fears eating it. He cannot bring himself to eat it. His eyes are still on the baby. He wants to tell Guddi that he has killed one just like it.

She knows. She knows what he has done.

Or she will find out in the days to come. Everyone will talk about the burning of a family in Shaan Gulley, and she will understand his part in it because Anand Bhai called him a hero.

Chamdi watches the baby's belly move up and down as it breathes. The other baby . . . Hanif's baby . . . it must have been sleeping too. No, he reminds himself. He heard the baby's wail from inside the house. It was wide awake.

Something is clawing at his heart. He does not know how to make it stop.

Perhaps he should speak to Guddi, tell her exactly what he has done.

No, he will never tell her. He knows Guddi is watching his every move. He is glad. He has been forced to commit a horrific act because of her.

Let her watch.

The moment he thinks this, he is ashamed. He must not blame her for what has happened. Sumdi or Guddi would have done the same for him.

Guddi leans over and steadies his hand. He did not even realize that it was shaking. He immediately takes his hand away from hers—it is the same hand that held the bottle.

"Whatever happened, it will be okay," she whispers to him. "It's okay."

It will never be okay, he thinks.

"Come with me," says Guddi. "I want to take you somewhere."

Chamdi lies on the ground and closes his eyes. There is no use in going with her. No matter where she takes him, the flames of Shaan Gulley will always follow him.

SIXTEEN

A taxiwala's car stereo plays an old Hindi song. As Chamdi walks, he looks in through the front window of the parked taxi, at a string of white jasmines that hangs from the rear-view mirror. Then he looks at the garland in his hand and tells himself that the one he holds is special. Not because it is made of marigolds and lilies, but because he has made it himself. He has made it for Sumdi.

Guddi has been wanting to bring Chamdi here for a while now. The only reason he has finally agreed to go with her today is because it was exactly a month ago that Sumdi died. But in the days that have passed, Chamdi has hardly spoken.

As they take the bend towards the Taj Mahal Hotel, crows caw in the trees. Through their branches, Chamdi can see the sky, a shy tinge of orange. In the dawn, the *tring-tring* of a milkman's cycle can be heard. He trudges past them in khaki shorts and a blue shirt, a steel container hanging from the side of his cycle.

As they approach the sea wall, Chamdi notices the Gateway of India in front of him. He sees the brown structure, its four turrets, its central archway, and he wonders why it was built. The Taj Mahal Hotel opposite resembles an old palace, its corners flanked by orange domes, a larger dome in the middle. Pigeons chatter away on the white arches of windows and some flutter alongside its stone walls. Uniformed cleaners hum to themselves and mop the concrete steps of the hotel. To the right of the hotel, coconut trees line the compounds of residential buildings, and even though the buildings look old, their balconies are spacious, and they seem strong.

Around Chamdi, women sweepers clean up the night's garbage with thick straw brooms and old men walk by the sea wall in white shorts. A man with a curling moustache sits on his haunches with a kerosene stove by his side and sells chai in small paper cups. Stray dogs and pigeons share the footpath along with beggars, and a man without legs is asleep in his hand-operated wheelchair. A bus driver stands outside his blue tourist bus with an incense stick in his hand, which he circles round and round, and chants a prayer in a low, heavy voice. Chamdi wants to say a prayer too, for Hanif the taxiwala, but he closes his eyes and asks Hanif to forgive him instead.

"I used to come here with my father," says Guddi. "We used to sit here all day and eat chana. This is my favourite place in Bombay."

Guddi sits on the sea wall and dangles her feet over the edge, the water below her. She looks at Chamdi and he knows she wants him to do the same. As he takes his place beside her, the sun sends its soft glow all around. This area is very different from anything Chamdi has seen. There is so much space, the sea does not seem to end.

Chamdi feels the garland in his hands. The old woman has taught him to leave just the right amount of space between the flowers so that they can breathe. He liked it when she told him that. In a few hours, he will go to Darzi's room, sit on the floor with a basket full of marigolds and lilies by his side, and thread garlands.

He looks towards the horizon and thinks of Sumdi. By now, Sumdi must have fulfilled his dream. He must have visited every single corner of Bombay, witnessed every cricket match, bet at every gambling den. Sumdi's words rush to him: *Then I will fly over the sea like a champion bird, and never ever stop.* Even though the sea is so vast, Sumdi would cross it in no time. Who knows, he might even have a beedi in his mouth.

Chamdi has made this garland for Sumdi because he never had a chance to say goodbye. When the flames ate Sumdi's body, all Chamdi did was watch. He hopes Sumdi forgives him. With this thought, Chamdi throws the garland into the sea. The garland moves farther and farther away. Where will the sea take it? he wonders. He wishes Guddi and he could float away in the same manner, to whatever country lies on the other side.

"Sometimes I dream Sumdi is in our village," says Guddi, "and he's pretending he cannot walk. Just for fun."

Chamdi says nothing. He listens to the chatter of pigeons and is reminded of the orphanage wall. Perhaps by now the orphanage has already been destroyed. He hopes everyone is okay, especially Mrs. Sadiq and Pushpa.

"Chamdi, please talk to me," says Guddi. "So what if we work for Anand Bhai? We are still good, no?"

He raises his head a little and catches a glimpse of her feet, the cracks lined with dirt, then at the brown dress that sits in her lap, loose and ill fitting, then at the orange bangles she never takes off, but he is unable to look any higher—at her face, into her eyes.

"Chamdi, you must talk to me," she says. "You hardly talk to me." Her voice begins to crack.

But he just stares at the water, at the small boats that sway from side to side. The sweeper's broom makes a rustling sound behind them. The panting of dogs can also be heard.

Chamdi faces the horizon and runs his hands across his ribs. They are as sharp as ever, but he now knows that they will never transform into tusks. Nor will police-tigers emerge from the blue-and-yellow stripes of police station walls. He will have to find other ways to protect Guddi.

But he has nothing to hold on to. When he left the orphanage, he had Kahunsha. He saw it so clearly, like it was real, as though it did truly exist. Now even his bougainvilleas are of no use.

He hears Guddi take a deep breath. He still does not look her way because if she is crying, he will not be able to do much.

But Guddi begins to sing.

Her voice takes Chamdi by surprise, and for a moment, he watches the water directly below him gently push itself against the sea wall. Guddi's voice is soft at first, but when it rises, he is reminded of the beauty in her song the first time he heard it, and he knows that even though she is sitting right next to him, she is far, far away.

He looks into the distance, at the manner in which the sea and sky meet as though they are friends. Soon the sea will nudge the sun into the sky, and the sea might do the same with her song so that it can reach her father, and even Sumdi.

But he feels that she is singing for him. He wonders how Guddi can bring herself to sing for him even though it is she who has lost a brother. She has hardly cried, and it might be because she wants Chamdi to feel better. He wonders where she gets the strength.

Chamdi looks at the way in which her left hand is outstretched in front of her, as though she is showing her voice where to go. She is guiding her voice over the water, and by the sway of her hand, her voice will know what waves to jump over and which ones to crash into. Her orange bangles clink into each other as she does this, and he traces his way up her elbow, to the sleeve of her dress, when he notices her chest.

Guddi sings with so much power that her chest heaves up and down.

While it is her voice that travels seawards, it is her chest that releases her song.

That is where her song comes from. That is where her strength lies.

At that moment, Chamdi feels something move within his chest too.

He tells himself that it could be anything.

Perhaps it is a police-tiger.

Yes, the police-tigers are inside his chest, and even though they are silent now, someday they will roar. Someday he will let them out.

He wants to tell her this as her voice soars above the waves.

Just then, he hears a sound. It is the gallop of horses, mad and strong. All of Bombay's horse carriages are by the sea, and that in itself is an unusual sight, but what dazzles Chamdi is the nature of the horses themselves. They are made from bougainvillea, every vein and fibre of these magnificent beasts is flower. They race towards the sea wall, jump over the astonished heads of men and women, into the water.

This makes Chamdi's heart race. He takes a deep breath.

He watches as the sun slowly takes its place in the sky and sends its light around in a sparkling dance.

Behind him, there is the sudden flutter of pigeons, as though they have all flown away at the same time.

As the water gurgles beneath them, Chamdi moves closer to Guddi, and lets his hand touch hers.

ACKNOWLEDGEMENTS.

My deepest gratitude to God and the Bhavnagris for their guidance and blessings.

To my friends Shiamak, Nakul, Glen, Rohan, Marzi, Puneet, Rajesh and Riyaaz for being good listeners and making invaluable suggestions.

To my agent, Denise Bukowski, for being a wonderful guardian of my work.

To my editor, Maya Mavjee, for her faith and wisdom.

A special thank you to Daniel Slager, Hilary Reeves, Emily Cook, and everyone at Milkweed for believing in this story.

Anosh Irani was born and brought up in Bombay, India and moved to Vancouver in 1998. He is the author of the acclaimed novel *The Cripple and His Talismans*. His first play, *The Matka King*, premiered at the Arts Club Theatre Company, Vancouver, in 2003. His most recent play, *Bombay Black*, commissioned and developed by Nightswimming, was produced by Cahoots Theatre Projects, Toronto, in 2006 and won four Dora Awards, including Outstanding New Play.

MILKWEED EDITIONS.

Founded in 1979, Milkweed Editions is one of the largest independent, nonprofit, literary publishers in the United States. Milkweed publishes with the intention of making a humane impact on society, in the belief that good writing can transform the human heart and spirit. Within this mission, Milkweed publishes in four areas: fiction, nonfiction, poetry, and children's literature for middle grade readers.

JOIN US.

Milkweed depends on the generosity of foundations and individuals like you, in addition to the sales of its books. In an increasingly consolidated and bottom-line driven publishing world, your support allows us to select and publish books on the basis of their literary quality and the depth of their message. Please visit our Web site (www.milkweed.org) or contact us at (800) 520–6455 to learn more about our donor program.